For my loving wife who's strength and support never waivers.

BOUNDLESS DESIRE

A Couple's Journey of Love, Lust, & Exploration

By C. L. Tummel

This is a work of fiction. Similarities to real people, places, or events are entirely coincidental.

BOUNDLESS DESIRE

First edition. March 31, 2024.

Copyright © 2024 C. L. Tummel.

ISBN: 979-8224923502

Written by C. L. Tummel.

PART I

INITIATION

CHAPTER 1

Steven and Dana McCormick sat together, arms linked and smiles on their faces, appearing as a picture-perfect couple with their athleisure outfits and unassuming appearance. Their home is immaculate, with every item in its place and not a speck of dust in sight.

They reside in a charming suburban home with white picket fences and neatly trimmed hedges. However, hidden behind closed doors was a burning desire that fueled their every thought and movement. Their lustful gazes and subtle touches betrayed their seemingly conventional façade, hinting at the wild desires brewing beneath the surface. Their home, filled with polished furniture and tidy décor, held secrets waiting to be unleashed. Every room held potential for passion and exploration, just waiting for the right moment to ignite.

On this particular evening, as they sat in the living room of home, Steven turned to Dana and confessed his deepest longing. Steven reached out, his fingers brushing against Dana's as she set her glass back onto the coffee table. The contact was fleeting but electric, sparking a warmth that flickered in his chest and spread quickly through his veins. He observed the way her laugh lines crinkled around those vibrant green eyes, a testament to the years of shared joy between them. Those eyes had always been his anchor, deep pools where he found solace and wild excitement in equal measure.

"Trying to distract me?" Dana quipped, her voice laced with humor and an edge of challenge.

"Is it working?" Steven's grin was boyish, his voice a low timbre that held a note of genuine curiosity.

"Maybe," she conceded, allowing the corner of her mouth to curve upward. She leaned into him, her body fitting against his like two perfect pieces of a puzzle long completed. Her scent enveloped him—a blend of vanilla and something uniquely Dana—earthy and intoxicating.

"Good." His hand rose, hovering just above the arch of her hip before settling there, a silent affirmation of his admiration for the woman who'd captivated him since their first encounter. "You know," he murmured, guiding her gently to sit beside him on the plush couch, "you never cease to amaze me."

"Well, I am pretty amazing," Dana replied. Their gazes locked, each reflecting years of understanding, of laughter and passion, and the countless quiet moments that had woven the fabric of their marriage into something resilient and beautiful.

"Your strength," Steven continued, his thumb caressing the soft material of her sweater at her side, "your sassiness, your fire—it's all still so damn enthralling."

Dana blushed, a rare show of bashfulness from a woman so typically confident. She tucked a stray lock of blonde hair behind her ear, revealing the delicate contour of her neck. "You're not so bad yourself, Mister," she said, her voice dropping to a whisper that carried the weight of their history, of secrets shared and boundaries crossed together.

Their laughter mingled, a sound as familiar and comforting as the heartbeat of their home. With a playful shove, Dana nudged Steven, a silent gesture that spoke volumes of the trust and camaraderie that underpinned their relationship.

"Come here," he said softly, wrapping an arm around her shoulders, pulling her close. Dana rested her head against his chest, listening to the steady rhythm of his heart, a beat that had become her favorite melody over the years.

In that embrace, they found a haven, a place where the world outside faded into insignificance, leaving only the certainty of their bond. And as the daylight waned, casting long shadows across the room, their connection remained a beacon, illuminating the depth of their commitment and the fervor of their love.

Dana nestled deeper into the embrace of the oversized couch; her gaze fixed on the dancing flames in the fireplace. The warmth of the fire mirrored the comfort of their living room—a sanctuary that had witnessed the evolution of their love over the years. Steven sat opposite her; an unreadable expression etched upon his face as he nursed a glass of red wine between his fingers.

"Steven?" Dana's voice sliced through the silence, tinged with curiosity at his prolonged quiet. "What are you thinking about?"

He hesitated for a moment, his eyes searching hers before settling back on the gentle swirl of his drink. The flickering light cast shadows across his features, hinting at the internal debate that seemed to hold him captive. Finally, he set the glass down on the coffee table with a soft clink and drew in a deep breath.

"Dana, we've always been honest with each other, right?" Steven's voice was steady, but there was an undercurrent of something new, something uncharted.

"Always," she replied, a slight frown creasing her brow at the solemnity in his tone.

"You know the fantasy I've continued to harbor for some time now," he began, his words deliberate. "I can't seem to get it out of my head or my dreams."

Dana felt her pulse quicken, a cocktail of and wariness and dread bubbling within her. She could almost feel the weight of his confession before he'd even spoken it.

"You know I want to watch you," he continued, his gaze unwavering. "I want to see you being pleasured by another man."

The words lingered in the air, imbuing everything with a bitter fragrance. Dana's heart raced, trying to comprehend what had just been revealed. This wasn't the first time they had explored this topic, and it never ended well before.

Her words caught in her throat as she tried to find the right ones. She was speechless, caught off guard by his request. Conflicting emotions raged inside her; shock at the boldness of the ask, a slight sense of flattery, and a hint of fear at what it could do to them if they crossed that line again.

Steven spoke up, sensing her silence as distress. "I don't want you to take this the wrong way," he interjected. "This isn't about feeling unsatisfied or lacking anything; it's about exploring our desires together. We talked about this before but I don't think we were in the right place, mentally or emotionally, and honestly, I don't think our relationship was strong enough at the time to handle something like this."

Dana looked at him, really looked, and saw not just her husband but the man who had always dared to push the limits of their love, always with her hand firmly in his. Steven's eyes held a mixture of hope and vulnerability, a silent plea for understanding.

She reached out, her fingers brushing against his, a gesture laden with the complexity of their shared history. This was not a demand but an invitation, one that required careful navigation. Love and trust had been the cornerstones of their relationship, and whatever step they took next would need to be built on the same foundation.

"We need to talk about this more, Steven. I need to understand." Her voice was steady now, the initial shock giving way to a cautious openness as she prepared to delve deeper into the unspoken depths of her partner's longing.

The last rays of the setting sun cast a warm glow over the living room, where Dana and Steven nestled into their usual evening repose. Amidst the casual setting, their fluffy, ever loyal Benny was draped across Steven's lap. The television murmured in the background, a forgotten narrative as their own story unfolded in hushed tones.

"Steven?" Dana's voice was hesitant, a delicate thread wavering in the silence that followed his unexpected confession. His gaze, once filled with unmistakable adoration, now held a flicker of something new, something uncharted. "Are you serious?" she asked, her heartbeat quickening against the calm cadence of their intertwined hands.

He nodded slowly, his eyes not leaving hers. "I've thought about it a lot," he admitted, his voice steady yet laced with an undercurrent of vulnerability. "Watching you, Dana, experiencing pleasure from another angle... It excites me. It's not about wanting less of you—it's about seeing you in a new, and different light, a new ecstasy."

Dana's breath caught in her throat, her mind racing to process his request. The warmth of his tone couldn't stave off the sudden chill that swept through her. This was a side of Steven she didn't appreciate, a depth of desire she had known existed within the man whose soul seemed so interwoven with her own.

"Another man?" The words fell from her lips before she could catch them, each syllable heavy with disbelief and a twinge of fear. Her green eyes, usually so full of laughter and life, now searched his for reassurance, for the foundation they had built together.

"I think we can handle it this time," Steven hastened to add, squeezing her hand gently, a lifeline thrown amidst the waves of uncertainty that crashed around them. "We don't have to do anything you're not comfortable with. And you don't have to worry about us, I love you, Dana. That's never going to change."

Her chest tightened as she withdrew slightly, trying to make sense of the tumultuous thoughts vying for attention. Surprise, curiosity, a sense of trepidation—all jostled within her. Was it possible for her to indulge in such a daydream? Would this instance prove to be different from the previous ones? Could their bond truly withstand the potential danger or disruption?

"Steven, I..." She trailed off, the conclusion of her sentence lost in a sea of indecision. Would delving into this fantasy build new bonds of trust within their marriage, or unravel the intricate patterns they had so lovingly crafted?

In the stillness of their cozy living room, the question hung in the air, a silent specter of what could be—an invitation to an unknown realm that promised both thrill and threat. And as nightfall embraced them with its darkening embrace, Dana knew that whatever path they chose, they would navigate it together.

iii

Dana sank into the plush cream sofa, her heart aflutter with a mix of trepidation and curiosity. Steven sat next from her, his expression a blend of hope and concern. The air between them crackled with the weight of the conversation they'd just had.

"Steven," Dana began, her voice barely above a whisper but carrying the strength of her burgeoning resolve, "I won't pretend that I'm not... intrigued but..." She paused, searching his eyes, "but if it's something you truly desire, I think I'm willing to explore it —with careful steps."

Steven's face softened, his eyes alight with a mixture of relief and excitement. "Really?" he asked, the word laced with cautious optimism.

"Yes," she affirmed. Her own curiosity surprised her; it was like peering through a keyhole to glimpse a secret garden. Seductive. Forbidden. And yet, somehow inviting.

"Okay then," Steven slid closer to her on the sofa. His proximity was reassuring, his warmth a familiar comfort. "We need to be on the same page about every detail. Communication is key. We didn't do a good job of discussing our expectations in the past." He took her hand in his, an anchor in the swirling sea of possibility.

"No, we certainly did not," Dana agreed, feeling the solidity of their bond, the foundation upon which they could build this new experience. "It needs to be someone who understands this is about us, our connection."

"Someone who respects our rules and boundaries," Steven added, his thumb caressing the back of her hand gently.

"Exactly. And how do we even start looking for... that person?" Dana's voice faltered slightly, the practicalities of the situation daunting.

"Carefully," Steven said with a smile that didn't quite reach his eyes. "There are communities, discreet channels where we can find what we're looking for. But we'll vet them together, make sure they're the right fit before anything happens."

"Ok," Dana nodded, feeling a surge of empowerment at the idea of having control over the situation. "This is about us, our pleasure. Our adventure."

"Always," Steven confirmed, pulling her into a tender embrace.

"Then let's take the first step," Dana said as she rested her head against his chest, listening to the steady rhythm of his heartbeat. It was a lifeline, a reminder that no matter how far they wandered in search of fantasy, they were anchored to each other.

"Tomorrow," Steven whispered, kissing the top of her head. "We'll start tomorrow."

And with that promise, they edged closer to the brink of an exhilarating journey, hand in hand, hearts entwined.

iv

Dana's fingers traced the rim of her glass, the cool surface mirroring the chill of uncertainty that had settled in her chest. Yet, as she raised her eyes to meet Steven's, a spark of something else flickered in their depths—curiosity. It was an ember, warm and dangerous, threatening to ignite into a blaze that could consume them both. Or perhaps it would illuminate a path previously untraveled.

"Tell me more," she began, her voice soft but not weak. "About how you see this... fantasy unfolding."

Steven's lips curved into a tentative smile, relief ebbing through his features like sunlight breaking through overcast skies. He leaned closer, his voice a conspiratorial whisper that tickled her ear and sent an unexpected shiver down her spine.

"Firstly," he murmured, "we need to find someone we trust implicitly. Someone who understands this is about us, about enhancing what we have, not replacing or diminishing it."

Dana nodded slowly, absorbing his words, letting them swirl around her mind like wine in her glass. Trust was their bedrock, the foundation upon which they had built a decade of love, laughter, and lust. To bring another into their sanctuary, they would need to fortify that foundation with clear and open communication.

"Someone who respects our boundaries," she added, her own vision for this escapade beginning to take shape. "We'll set the rules, the dos and don'ts. And if either of us feels uncomfortable at any point..."

"We stop," Steven finished for her, squeezing her hand. "No questions asked. Our marriage comes first. Always."

"Always," she echoed, the word feeling like a vow.

They sat in silence for a moment, each lost in contemplation. Dana felt the weight of her reservations, heavy like velvet drapes, but the allure of the unknown tugged at her with silken threads. The idea of being desired, of being seen through fresh eyes while still anchored to the love of her life, was intoxicating.

"Okay," Dana said finally, the word slicing through the tension. "We can explore this. Together. But we do it carefully, step by step. And you're right—we need someone who gets that."

"Absolutely," Steven agreed, his eyes alight with a mixture of excitement and adoration. "We'll take our time finding the right person. Someone who will honor the privilege of being invited into our world."

Their conversation turned to logistics, discussing potential scenarios and safeguards, all the while maintaining that essential thread of connection between them. Each word, every consideration, was a testament to their mutual respect and the strength of their bond.

As they talked, the embers of curiosity within Dana were stoked by their shared enthusiasm. What started as a hesitant flicker grew bolder, warmer. The anticipation of the unknown mingled with the safety of their love, crafting a potent cocktail of excitement and nerves.

"Whatever happens," Steven said, clasping her hands in his, "we're in this together. For better or for worse."

The room seemed to contract and expand with the magnitude of their decision. They were venturing into uncharted waters, but they would navigate them side by side, anchored by the love and trust they had built to become the bedrock of their marriage.

Dana and Steven eagerly scrolled through numerous websites, delving into the depths of swinger community chat rooms, fetish sites, and profiles. The descriptions ranged from tantalizingly explicit to surprisingly tame, each one igniting a spark of curiosity within the couple. They clicked through countless pictures, some showing daring acts of intimacy while others captured more subtle hints of desire and passion.

v

After what felt like an unending procession of individuals, carnal exchanges, and alluring cravings, they sat, knees touching, on the plush cream couch in their living room. The glow of the setting sun painted warm hues across the space, giving it an intimate atmosphere. In front of them on the coffee table lay the laptop open and showing a photograph, slightly blurred at the edges but clear enough to make out the features of the man pictured. His salt and pepper hair gave him a distinguished look, and even through the still image, there was an undeniable intensity in his dark eyes. Richard stood with confidence, the kind that came from years of knowing oneself, and an athletic build that hinted at both discipline and strength.

"Richard certainly has the... presence," Dana ventured carefully, her voice a mixture of trepidation and intrigue as she studied the photo.

Steven nodded, his hand finding hers and giving it an encouraging squeeze. "He does. And he's experienced in guiding couples who are fairly new to this. He understands the importance of communication, trust."

"Have you spoken to him much?" Dana asked, her gaze shifting from the photograph to Steven, searching for reassurance in his familiar green eyes.

"Enough to know he's serious about consent and discretion," Steven replied. "He's not just some thrill-seeker; he respects the sanctity of marriage. Ours especially."

Dana let out a breath she didn't realize she'd been holding. She felt the flutter again, that curious blend of nerves and excitement churning within her. "It's a big step," she whispered, almost to herself.

"Hey," Steven said softly, turning her chin towards him with a gentle finger. "We don't have to do anything we're not ready for. If we meet him and something feels off, we walk away. No harm, no foul."

"Promise?" Her green eyes searched his, looking for the anchor they had always provided.

"Promise." Steven kissed her forehead, the familiarity of his lips comforting. "We're in this together, remember? No matter what happens, we're a team."

"Team," she echoed with a faint smile, leaning into him. Their conversation flowed into silence, filled only by the soft creaking of the leather beneath them and the rhythmic ticking of the clock on the mantle. In the quiet, there was space for contemplation, for the weight of decisions yet to be made, and for the connection that bound them unyieldingly.

"Ok, if you're really sure," Dana finally said, her voice steady with resolved curiosity. "I'll send him a message confirming the details."

"Good," Steven affirmed. He watched her type, admiration shining in his eyes—not just for the woman she was, but for the woman she was continually becoming. This journey they were embarking on wasn't just about fulfilling fantasies; it was a reaffirmation of their bond, a promise to keep exploring the depths of their connection.

"Sent," Dana announced, returning to the couch with a renewed sense of purpose. Their eyes met; a silent pact made in a single glance.

"Saturday night then, at the JW Marriott bar," Steven confirmed, his thumb caressing the back of her hand. "No matter what, it's you and me, Dana. Always you and me."

"Always us," Dana agreed, the last rays of sunlight fading behind the horizon, leaving them enveloped in the soft lamplight, their shared future shimmering with potential as they braced themselves for the unknown.

vi

Each day dragged on like a slow torture, amplifying Dana and Steven's anticipation for the upcoming date with Richard. Their minds were consumed by wild fantasies and anxious thoughts, distracting them from their work. They couldn't shake off the growing sense of exhilaration and dread as they imagined what may unfold during their encounter with Richard. Would it be pleasure or pain? A fantasy come true or a nightmare in disguise? The uncertainty gnawed at their minds, making each passing moment feel like an eternity.

On the evening of their date, Dana stood at the bedroom window, her fingers absentmindedly tracing the cool glass of champagne she sipped as she watched the sun dip below the horizon. A soft sigh escaped her lips, the reflection of the room behind her catching her eye. The bed seemed to invite whispered secrets and unexplored pleasures, a silent witness to the countless intimacies she and Steven had shared—and now, potentially, another.

"Richard," she murmured, turning the name over in her mind like a smooth stone. He was the man they had found after days of cautious searching, a figure who represented both the fulfillment of Steven's fantasy and the expansion of their marital explorations. The image of him, pulled from the discreet online profile, lingered before her: a dominant presence with salt and pepper hair that spoke of experience but not age, and an athletic build that hinted at controlled power.

Dana stood before the open closet, her eyes scanning the sea of fabrics and colors. Richard's instructions had been explicit—something form-fitting and black, with a hint of red to symbolize the passion he anticipated kindling between them. She skimmed her fingertips over the smooth materials until they paused on the perfect outfit;

Dana stepped into the room, her outfit a perfect mix of seduction and sophistication. The form-fitting black dress clung to her curves like a second skin, while the lace lingerie peeking through added a hint of sensuality. Her stiletto heels clicked against the floor, making her presence known as she sauntered over with a sultry grace. The low light only enhanced the shimmer of her ensemble, commanding attention in every way possible.

She turned to face the full-length mirror. The silk embraced her like a lover's caress, tracing the line of her body in a way that made her feel both exposed and powerful. The color set off the golden tones in her hair, and the fabric shimmered with every movement, as if it were alive with the same anticipation that fluttered in her stomach.

"Wow," Steven's voice came from the doorway, rich with admiration. He leaned against the frame, his gaze drinking her in. "Richard might have given the instructions, but, Dana, you bring that dress to life."

Dana met his eyes in the reflection, a smile playing on her lips. His support was the steady flame that kept her own uncertainties at bay. "You're sure about this?" she asked, seeking confirmation one last time.

"Absolutely." Steven crossed the room, wrapping his arms around her from behind. His hands rested gently on her hips, thumbs brushing the silk as if to memorize the feel of it. "This is about us, remember? Exploring together. Whatever happens, it's about us."

She leaned back into his embrace, feeling the solid reassurance of his presence. "Together," she echoed, turning within his arms to face him. His eyes were filled with love and desire—a combination that had always been their unique alchemy.

"Besides," he added with a playful grin, "seeing you in that dress is going to make tonight unforgettable, no matter what."

"Unforgettable for you, or for Richard?" Dana teased, the lightness of their banter grounding her.

"Both," Steven said, his voice low, "but mostly for me. Because at the end of the night, it's you and I who will be leaving together, hearts still intertwined."

Dana turned away from the mirror, her heart somersaulting as she pondered the gravity of what lay ahead. The thought of another man, Richard, seeing her as Steven did—admiring, desiring—sent a shiver down her spine. She felt torn, caught between the safety of the love she knew and the thrilling precipice of the unknown.

"Hey," Steven said softly, approaching her. His hands settled on her shoulders, grounding her. "If there's any doubt, we don't go through with it. You know that, right?"

"I do," she answered, leaning back into his embrace. "It's just... it feels so big, so irrevocable."

"Everything we do is together, Dearest. Remember that." His voice was a soothing balm, yet it could not fully calm the storm of emotions within her. Loyalty, desire, fear, and curiosity swirled together, forming an intoxicating cocktail that left her heady. "Let's just meet him," Steven suggested, his thumb brushing the tension from her neck. "Talk to him, see how we feel. There's no pressure."

"Okay," Dana agreed, her resolve steeling even as her stomach fluttered with nerves. She could almost hear Richard's voice, deep and commanding, see the knowing look in his eyes as if he understood the power he held in his hands—the power to either enrich their bond or unravel it.

"Let's go then," Steven said, offering his hand. His touch was familiar and safe, a lifeline anchoring her amidst the waves of trepidation.

Dana took a deep breath, her decision settling around her like a second skin. She placed her hand in his, their fingers entwining—a silent vow to face whatever may come, together. With one last glance at the bed, the keeper of secrets, she stepped forward, ready to meet the man who might join them in writing a new chapter of their intimate tale.

The city lights blurred past as Steven navigated the sleek black car through the heart of downtown. Dana fidgeted with the hem of her dress, a whisper of silk against her thighs. She looked at Steven, his profile sharp against the backdrop of night, and took a measured breath.

"Steven, what do you hope will happen tonight?" Her voice was a mix of curiosity and an edge of excitement.

Steven glanced at her, the corners of his mouth lifting in a half-smile that didn't quite mask the thrum of his own anticipation. "I think it's not just about what happens, but how we experience it together. I want us to find new edges of our desires, to push boundaries safely."

Dana nodded, considering his words. The idea of Richard joining them had been like a match struck in the dark - surprising and illuminating. "And if it becomes too much?" she asked, the vulnerability of the question hanging between them.

"Then we stop," Steven said firmly, reaching over to squeeze her hand. "This is about us, Dana. Our pleasure, our choice. We're in this together."

"Right. Together." The word felt like a talisman in her mouth, something powerful and binding. Their shared gaze in the rear-view mirror held a promise, a silent pact that whatever the night brought, it would be theirs to own.

Dana's heart pounded in her chest with a mixture of trepidation and excitement as Steven pulled into the valet area.

vii

"Ready?" he asked, his voice carrying an undercurrent of anticipation that mirrored her own.

Dana nodded silently, smoothing the fabric of her dress—a garment chosen not by herself but by Richard, the man they were about to meet. She stepped out of the car, her heels clicking authoritatively against the pavement. The evening breeze flirted with the hem of her black dress, which clung to her like a lover's embrace, hinting at the secrets of her curves without giving too much away.

The plunging neckline left little to the imagination regarding her ample breasts, while the slit along the side of the dress promised glimpses of her toned legs with every step she took. It was a bold choice, one that commanded attention, and as she walked beside Steven towards the hotel bar, she felt every bit the object of desire that Richard intended her to be.

The bar exuded a mysterious aura, with its deep blue walls and layers of moody white lighting. The focal point was the imposing dark bar, standing like an island amidst the intimately placed booths and dimly lit candle-lit tables. As soon as one stepped into this hidden retreat, they were transported to another world, where secrets were shared over glasses of amber liquid and eclectic soft music hummed in the background. It was a place for contemplation and indulgence, where time seemed to stand still in the mesmerizing atmosphere.

Patrons turned their heads as the couple entered, the atmosphere of the bar charged with the subtle electric buzz of nightlife. Dana could feel the weight of eyes upon her, assessing and admiring, as she moved gracefully across the room. Steven's hand rested lightly on the small of her back, both a symbol of support and a silent claim to her affections.

The air was perfumed with the scent of expensive cologne and the warmth of whiskey as they approached the spot where they were to meet Richard. Each step Dana took was measured, her confidence building with the knowledge that tonight, she was the embodiment of a fantasy brought vividly to life.

viii

Dana's pulse thrummed in her ears; a rhythm that quickened with each step closer to the bar. The cacophony of the JW Marriott's nightlife was a distant murmur compared to the tempest of emotions swirling within her. Her hand rested in Steven's, a lifeline anchoring her to the moment.

"Hey," Steven said softly, giving her hand a gentle squeeze. "You're doing that thing where you chew on your lip. Talk to me."

The concern in his voice felt like a warm blanket, and she let out a breath she didn't realize she'd been holding. "It's just... this is real now, isn't it? Meeting Richard, it's not fantasy anymore." Her words came out more vulnerable than she intended.

Steven stopped, turning to face her, his expression earnest and full of love. "Dana, if at any point you want to stop—"

"No," she cut him off, her resolve firming. "I want this. I want to see where this path leads us." But the fluttering in her stomach belied her confident words, revealing the dance of her loyalty and personal desires.

"Okay, then we'll take it one step at a time, together." His thumb traced circles on the back of her hand, grounding her.

Together. That word again. It was their strength, their mantra. With a deep inhale, Dana allowed herself to feel the thrill that came with the unknown, letting it seep into her bones until it was a part of her as much as her own breath.

They resumed their walk, the noise of the hotel bar growing clearer with every step. Laughter rang out like chimes in the wind, the soundscape of high spirits and loose inhibitions. The clink of ice against glass, the soft hum of the music mingling with the din, it all painted a picture of a world teetering on the edge of decadence.

As they approached the bar, the air seemed to vibrate with a potent mix of excitement and apprehension. Dana's gaze swept over the patrons, each person a story yet to unravel. And there, amidst the tapestry of faces, stood Richard. His presence was like a beacon, drawing them inexorably forward.

Steven leaned in, his lips brushing against her ear. "Ready for an adventure?"

"As I'll ever be," she replied, her voice steady with newfound determination, even as her heart raced with the promise of the night's uncharted territory.

Their fingers intertwined, Dana and Steven stepped through the threshold of the bar, crossing into a new chapter of their life together—one filled with the tantalizing scent of possibility.

CHAPTER 2

Amidst the dim ambiance of the bar, a singular figure commanded presence without uttering a single word. Richard stood in front of a secluded booth; his posture relaxed yet exuding undeniable authority. The low lighting cast shadows that played across his angular features, his piercing gaze cutting through the haze as he surveyed his surroundings with an air of ownership.

As Dana and Steven navigated through the clusters of patrons, their steps were tentative, weighted with a cocktail of nervousness and intrigue. Richard's eyes locked onto them long before they had reached his domain, and the intensity of his stare sent a shiver down Dana's spine.

Richard was dressed impeccably in a tailored suit that seemed to mold to his frame, accentuating broad shoulders and a statuesque build. His hair, dark and meticulously groomed, framed a face that was both handsome and inscrutable. There was something about him that whispered danger, yet his charismatic smile, when it came, was disarmingly warm.

"Good evening," Richard's voice was a rich baritone that resonated with confidence, "Dana, Steven."

The moment Richard's gaze met hers, Dana felt the world shrink to the space between them. His smile widened just a fraction, but it was enough to convey he knew exactly the effort she had put into preparing for this encounter. Her cheeks flushed with a mix of embarrassment and excitement—an involuntary response to his silent acknowledgment.

"You look stunning," he said, his eyes lingering on Dana appreciatively. The compliment was simple, direct, yet it landed with the weight of a promise, sending a thrill through her body. The dress she wore, chosen with Richard's cryptic instructions in mind, suddenly felt like armor gilded with his approval.

"Thank you," Dana managed to respond, her voice steady despite the storm of anticipation swirling within her. She could feel Steven's supportive presence at her side, a grounding force amidst the charged atmosphere that Richard effortlessly conjured.

With a charming smile, Richard extended his arm towards the plush leather booth. "Please," he offered, "let's sit and order some drinks. I believe we have much to discuss." As if on cue, a server materialized by their side. "A glass of Veuve Sparkling Rose for the lovely lady and two Old Fashioneds for us, please," Richard requested with confidence. The bustling sounds of voices and clinking glasses filled the upscale lounge as they settled into the comfortably cushioned seats. The dim lighting cast a warm glow over their faces as they leaned in to begin their conversation.

ii

Dana settled into the booth, the leather cool against her bare thighs beneath the hem of her dress. She folded her hands in her lap, an attempt to still their trembling. To her right, Richard's presence was like a magnetic force, pulling her in with an energy that was as thrilling as it was intimidating.

"Relax," he murmured, his voice a low rumble that seemed to vibrate through her. It was a command wrapped in velvet, gentle yet firm. Dana nodded, though her heart raced like a bird fluttering wildly in its cage.

Steven sat opposite them, his eyes searching hers for reassurance. She offered him a small smile, the unspoken communication between them a lifeline amidst the roiling sea of her emotions. In this venture, they were partners, but the uncharted waters they were about to navigate threatened the safe harbor of their relationship. The possibility of change, of something new and unknown, both excited and scared her.

"Let's talk about what tonight is going to look like," Richard said, his gaze holding both Dana and Steven as equals. He leaned forward, resting his forearms on the table, his fingers laced together, exuding control and confidence. "First, I want to know your limits," he continued, addressing Steven directly now, offering him the driver's seat in deciding how far they would go.

Steven cleared his throat, sharing a glance with Dana before speaking. "We're... open to exploring," Steven started, his voice steady but revealing a hint of the nerves Dana felt, "but we want to keep things... respectful. No one gets hurt."

"Of course," Richard nodded approvingly, his eyes flickering back to Dana. "And you, Dana? What are your desires for this evening?"

Dana swallowed, feeling the heat of Richard's gaze as if it were a physical touch. She wanted to be swept away, to experience the rush of surrender, yet the fear of the unknown clawed at the edges of her resolve.

"I want to push my boundaries," she admitted, her voice barely above a whisper, "but I need to know that I can trust you, that you'll stop if I say so."

"Absolutely," Richard assured her, his expression serious now. "You always have the power to say 'no'. Nothing happens without your consent."

The declaration seemed to hang in the air, heavy with the weight of the power exchange they were all agreeing to. Richard's eyes held hers, and Dana felt the last of her resistance crumble under the intensity of his gaze.

With furrowed brows and genuine curiosity, Steven leaned in and asked, "Please, can you give us some specific examples of how you think things should go? Your experience is invaluable to us." His voice was gentle but insistent, as if he didn't want to miss any important insights. "Is there anything we may have overlooked or not considered in our discussions so far?" The atmosphere in the room seemed to shift, with everyone eagerly awaiting a response that could potentially shape their decisions and actions moving forward.

With a confident smile, Richard spoke to the couple before him. "Throughout my experience working with couples, I have encountered those who sought me out as a dominant figure, while others simply desired my presence to enhance their lovemaking - whether through an additional set of hands or other means. Whatever your preference may be, I am well-versed and at ease in navigating any situation you desire." His words were calm and reassuring, putting the couple at ease as they considered their options.

Richard's eyes narrowed as he leaned in closer to Steven, his voice dripping with calculated intensity. "Just so I'm perfectly clear on your desires," he said, his words laced with a hint of malice. "You want to watch Dana without interfering like some kind of voyeuristic fly on the wall."

Steven swallowed nervously and nodded, feeling a chill run down his spine.

"Take heed, for what you are about to experience will challenge every belief you hold about reality. Your senses will be assaulted with sights that defy logic, sounds that reverberate through your very being, and emotions that threaten to overwhelm you. Yet, despite the intensity of it all, you will be nothing more than a silent observer, trapped in your seat as the events unfold before you." Richard's voice was filled with urgency. "Do you fully grasp the gravity of this?"

Staring back at Richard with wide eyes, Steven's face was flushed with a mixture of fear and excitement. His body language conveyed a sense of hesitation and uncertainty.

"Yes," Steven responded. "I understand."

Richard turned his gaze to Dana, who met it head on with steely determination. "And you," he said, his tone turning cold as ice, "want a taste of domination and submission. You crave pushing your limits and exploring the darker side." Dana's heart raced at the blunt assessment, but she couldn't deny the thrill that coursed through her veins. "Is that correct?" Richard repeated, his eyes boring into hers like lasers.

Dana nodded in silent agreement, her heart pounding in anticipation of what was to come.

"Good," he said, a smile playing on his lips once more. "Then let's begin."

CHAPTER 3

The low hum of conversation and the soft clinking of glasses in the dimly lit bar provided a discreet soundtrack to the private world that Richard, Dana and Steven had cocooned themselves within. Nestled together in their booth, the shadows played upon their features, granting them an air of secrecy and intrigue.

Dana could feel the warmth radiating from Richard's body as he leaned towards her, his posture relaxed yet deliberate. The closeness was intoxicating, making the space outside their bubble feel like a distant memory. She could smell the faintest hint of his cologne, a subtle scent that seemed to draw her in even closer.

"Steven," Richard stated, his voice firm and commanding. "This will be the last time I address you directly until our evening's proceedings have reached their end. After this point, your role will be one of observation - nothing more. Any further guidance, instruction, permission, consent, and conversation will solely occur between Dana and myself. Is that clear?" Steven nodded solemnly, comprehending the weight of Richard's words and his new role in the situation.

"Excellent," Richard confirmed with a nod, his voice steady and authoritative. "And Dana, although I will be taking the lead on our evening's activities, make no mistake - all of the power lies in your hands. You have the ultimate authority to stop at any time."

Dana swallowed nervously but nodded firmly, her confidence growing in spite of herself. "Yes, I understand," she replied, her gaze meeting Richard's with newfound determination.

Steven fidgeted in his seat, his heart racing with anticipation and fear. He didn't know what to expect from this encounter between his wife and the enigmatic stranger. Part of him wanted answers, but another part was afraid of what they might reveal. All he could do was wait and hope for the best.

"Your beauty is undeniable, Dana," Richard murmured, his voice a low purr that resonated with an undercurrent of desire. His breath was warm against her skin, each word spoken sending a tantalizing shiver along her spine.

She watched, almost as if in slow motion, as his hand moved with purposeful grace, his fingers lightly skimming over the bare skin of her arm. The light touch was more electric than she could have anticipated; it felt as though sparks were dancing upon her flesh, trailing a path of heat that awakened every nerve ending.

Each stroke of his touch seemed to speak volumes, promising unspoken pleasures and igniting a flame within her that she hadn't known could burn so fiercely. It was a dance of seduction played out through whispers and caresses, each one delicately balanced on the edge of propriety and passion.

ii

Dana's gaze, hesitant yet eager, met Richard's steady and penetrating stare. The dim light of the bar flickered in his eyes, casting a golden glow that seemed to pierce through her defenses. As their eyes locked, a crimson tide painted her cheeks, betraying the storm of excitement and nervousness swirling within her. She felt the undeniable magnetic pull of his presence, an attraction that tethered her to him with an invisible but iron-strong thread.

"I have many plans for us this evening, my dear," Richard hissed, his voice laced with a dark promise. "If you follow my instructions carefully, you will experience pleasures beyond your wildest imaginings. But if you dare to disobey me, or deviate from my commands in any way, you will suffer a much different sensation... one of pain and punishment." His eyes gleamed with a cruel glint as he spoke, and the air around them seemed to grow heavy with an ominous energy.

Across the booth, Steven's eyes darted between the two, captivated by the unfolding scene. His breath caught in his throat as he watched the interplay of emotions dance across Dana's face. With each passing second, his heart thudded against his ribcage, a relentless drumming fueled by a potent cocktail of arousal tinged with a sharp note of apprehension. He was a silent witness to the charged exchange, torn between the desire to intervene and the yearning to see where this tantalizing narrative would lead.

The subtle warmth of Richard's hand seeped through the fabric of Dana's dress as his fingers began their deliberate ascent up her thigh. Each brush was a stroke of deliberate artistry, igniting trails of heat that spiraled inward and upward, threatening to unravel the composure she clung to so fiercely. She could feel her pulse quicken, punctuating the silence that enveloped them with its insistent rhythm.

Richard leaned in, his breath a warm whisper against the shell of her ear, sending a shiver cascading down her spine. "Imagine the ecstasy waiting to be discovered," he murmured, his voice low and laced with promise. "I want to explore every hidden desire with you, unfold each layer of your passion until you're awash in pleasure."

Dana's response was caught in her throat, a gasp that mingled fear with longing. The words hung between them, an invitation that tugged at her with the gravity of a forbidden fruit. Her resolve wavered like a flame in a gentle breeze, each of Richard's seductive promises fanning it into a blaze. She felt herself drawn dangerously close to the precipice of surrender, teetering on the edge of an adventure her heart yearned to embark upon.

Steven's breath caught, the sight before him a potent mix of voyeuristic thrill and profound affection. From his vantage point, he watched Richard's hand become a silhouette against the low light of the booth, a shadow play that hinted at the tender exploration happening beneath. Dana's chest rose and fell with a rhythm that spoke of deepening desire; her lips parted ever so slightly as if in silent plea for more.

In the dimly lit bar, Richard's fingers traced the outline of Dana's thigh, gliding up her smooth skin until they reached the hem of her dress. He could feel the throb of desire emanating from between her legs, and he couldn't resist the urge to explore further. His hand slid underneath her dress, pushing aside the delicate layer of lace to reveal her glistening wetness. Dana let out a soft gasp as his fingers began to stroke and caress her, sending shivers of pleasure through her body. Steven, sitting across from them, could see the telltale signs of arousal on Dana's trembling shoulders, her body giving in to the primal desires that needed no verbal communication.

The playful glint in Richard's eye was unmistakable, even in the dim glow of the candle flickering on their table.

"Mmm...that's it, my dear," Richard purred, his voice sending shivers down her spine. "Open yourself up to the endless possibilities of this evening. I can see you're eager to explore where our passions will take us." His eyes burned into hers with a hungry intensity, making her stomach churn with nervous excitement.

He playfully traced his fingertips along the delicate, slick petals nestled between her thighs, causing her body to tingle with desire. Every nerve was on fire as he teased her sensitive flesh, building up a delicious ache that begged for release. She moaned and arched her hips in response to his cunning touch, desperate for more of his expert caresses. Dana tilted her head back, exposing the column of her throat to the warmth of the bar-laced air, a silent surrender to the sensation.

Richard's voice was deep and velvety, sending shivers down her spine. "Mmm," he murmured, his words laced with desire. She could feel it emanating from him, a palpable force that drew her closer. "There is no use trying to hide it," he breathed, his gaze burning into hers. The air between them crackled with unspoken passion as he leaned in, his lips almost brushing against hers. In that moment, she knew her resolve was slipping away.

Steven's pulse thrummed in his ears, a symphony to the erotic tableau unfolding before him. The sight of another man's hand tracing the contours of Dana's body, however subtly, stoked a fire within him that bordered on primal. The possessiveness that should have flared within him was instead replaced by a fervent wish to witness her pleasure, to be the custodian of her fulfillment in ways traditional bounds would not allow.

Dana's eyes fluttered closed, her lashes casting crescent shadows upon her cheeks as Richard's fingertips continued their dance. With each deliberate caress, a soft moan threatened to escape her lips, a testament to the smoldering desire that coursed through her veins.

In this charged atmosphere, Steven felt the very fabric of their relationship subtly shift, morphing into something beautifully uncharted. It was as if they were all players in an intimate ballet; each movement, each breath, each lingering touch composed a choreography of sensuality that promised an awakening of new desires.

iii

The heat from Richard's fingertips seared her skin. A gasp caught in her throat, a delicate sound that hovered between temptation and restraint. She could feel Steven's eyes on them, heavy with longing and silent encouragement, yet a tremor of hesitation quivered within her.

"Beautiful," Richard murmured, his voice velvet and danger intertwined. His fingers paused; the question clear in their stillness: How far are you willing to let this go?

Dana's heart hammered against her ribcage, a frantic drumbeat echoing her internal clash. Loyalty to Steven, a steadfast pillar in her life, vied with the surging current of desire that Richard elicited with each calculated move. Her mind spun with visions of entwined bodies and whispered secrets, but Steven's presence anchored her, a lifeline amidst the storm of passion that Richard stirred.

"Perhaps we might find a more... private setting?" Richard's voice had dropped to a husky whisper that caressed her ear, sending shivers cascading down her spine. His gaze, heavy-lidded and expectant, locked onto hers, reading her like the pages of an open book, waiting to be devoured.

The proposition hung in the air between them, a tangible invitation laced with the promise of pleasure. Dana's breath hitched, her lips parting slightly as she weighed the precipice of decision. The look in Richard's eyes was patient yet filled with a desire that mirrored the fire he had ignited within her.

In that moment, Dana understood the powerful allure of the forbidden, the thrill of stepping outside the lines drawn by society, by herself. Richard's suggestion wasn't merely a change of location; it was an offer to explore the depths of her own sensuality, with Steven's silent blessing fueling her courage.

She swallowed hard, her pulse racing with the possibilities that lay beyond the threshold of the awaiting hotel room.

Steven's pulse quickened, the thrumming in his veins a chaotic symphony as he watched the silent exchange. The flickering candlelight cast an ethereal glow on Dana's face, accentuating the soft contours that he knew so well, yet now they were etched with a new, unfamiliar tension. Her chest rose and fell in shallow breaths, her lips slightly parted as if to speak, but no words came.

The air around them was thick with anticipation, every second stretching out like an eternity. He could almost taste the intoxicating blend of desire and fear that emanated from her, the same emotions that mirrored his own internal battle. This was his fantasy unfolding before him, yet the thudding in his chest reminded him that it was also Dana's reality to confront.

Dana's gaze flickered, a storm of thoughts passing behind her eyes. The allure of Richard's proposition tugged at her, a magnetic pull toward the unknown, toward uncharted pleasures that beckoned with the sweet promise of ecstasy. But beneath that temptation lay a bedrock of trepidation; each heartbeat a stark reminder of the love she shared with Steven; of the life they had built together.

Within that dimly lit booth, Dana stood at the precipice of choice, each breath a measured step toward a destination yet unknown. Her fingers traced the edge of the table, the cool surface grounding her even as her mind spun through a maelstrom of what-ifs and maybes. Richard's presence loomed beside her, a catalyst for the awakening desires that simmered just below the surface, threatening to boil over and scald all reason.

Steven felt a surge of excitement ripple through him, a voyeur to the inner turmoil that played across his wife's features. His own desires, once a whisper within him, now roared like a tempest, eager to witness the fruition of their shared fantasy. Yet, as he observed the dance of emotions on Dana's face, he couldn't ignore the pang of protectiveness that clutched at his heart.

With each ragged breath, Dana's decision teetered on the edge of a knife, poised between the safety of the known and the dizzying potential of the night ahead. Her heart, a frenzied drummer in the quiet bar, pounded out a rhythm that seemed to resonate with the very fabric of her being. It was a cacophony of longing and fear, of love and lust, playing a duet that only she could harmonize.

In the stillness, Steven's gaze remained locked on Dana, the air between them charged with unspoken words and shared history. The weight of the moment bore down upon them, a pressure that tested the bonds of trust and the resilience of their connection. And amidst the shadows and whispers of the bar, Dana's resolve crystallized, her decision made manifest in the subtle nod that sealed their fates, entwining them in the tapestry of an evening that promised to redefine the contours of their desires.

iv

The pulse of the bar's dim lights cast a subtle glow on Dana, reflecting like distant stars in her widening eyes. Richard's gaze, intense yet gentle, held hers with an unwavering steadiness—a silent anchor amidst the storm of her inner turmoil. He was the embodiment of patience, his features softening with every hesitant beat of her heart.

"Take your time," Richard's voice flowed, barely above the thrum of the background music, but it resonated within Dana like a soothing balm. "There's no rush." His eyes, pools of dark promise, never strayed, assuring her that her boundaries were sacred, that her will was his command.

Across the booth, Steven watched the exchange, his love for Dana radiating from him in waves that seemed to ripple through the charged air. His unwavering gaze spoke volumes, each glance weaving a silent tapestry of support and unconditional trust. It was as if his eyes whispered, 'I am here. I am with you,' reinforcing the unbreakable bond they shared.

Their eyes met, and in that gaze, Dana found a fortress against her fears. With Steven's quiet strength bolstering her, she felt the vice of uncertainty loosen its grip. The connection between them, a testament to years of love and exploration, now expanded to include Richard in this delicate dance of desire.

In the space between heartbeats, Dana understood the depth of their union—it was not solely tethered to the physical but was an intricate weave of emotion and understanding that could endure even the most daring of adventures.

Dana's fingers curled around the stem of her wine glass, the cool surface grounding her as she drew in a deep, steadying breath. Her pulse quickened, each beat resonating through her body like the distant echo of a drum, heralding the momentous decision that lay before her. A thin veil of condensation blurred the edges of reality just enough to let her focus on the here and now, on the two sets of eyes that anchored her to this crossroads of desire.

She lifted her gaze, meeting Richard's expectant stare. His eyes, dark and deep, held a spark of adventure that beckoned her—a silent siren call to uncharted pleasures. The air between them hummed with the electricity of possibility, a current that danced upon her skin, teasing the hairs at the nape of her neck into awareness.

Richard's hand, warm and reassuring, rested lightly upon the table, an offer of companionship and more, his fingertips mere inches from hers. It was an invitation written in the language of touch—a language that Dana found herself increasingly fluent in under the tutelage of her own curiosity.

And then there was Steven. His presence, a constant ember of love that burned steadily amidst the whirlwind of emotions swirling within her. In his gaze, she read not only acceptance but encouragement—the embodiment of a love that did not chain but rather set free.

With her heart threading a symphony of yearning and fear, Dana mustered the courage that lived in the space where their gazes intertwined. It was time to step beyond the precipice of what was known and safe, time to plunge into the depths of what could be.

Her nod was subtle, almost imperceptible in the dim glow of the bar, yet it was as if she had declared her intent with the force of a thunderclap. Richard's lips twitched upwards in a knowing smile, one that promised to guide her through the labyrinth of sensation that awaited.

As her body trembled, a blend of exhilaration and nerves tingling across her skin, Dana felt as though she were shedding an old skin—revealing a version of herself that thrived on the adrenaline of the unknown. Tonight, she realized, was not just another evening. It was the beginning of an odyssey that would redefine the boundaries of her pleasure, her trust, and her very self.

"Let's go," she whispered, as much to Richard as to herself, sealing her resolve with the word that opened the gateway to a new horizon.

CHAPTER 4

Dana rose from the velvet cocoon of the booth, her limbs tremulous as though she were a fledgling about to take flight. Every nerve ending seemed alight with a treacherous cocktail of anxiety and yearning, rendering her steps uncertain and fluttery. Richard's hand was there, steady and enticing, an anchor in the storm of her senses. As he clasped her hand, a subtle yet undeniable strength transmitted through his touch, emboldening her to move forward.

The space between them closed as they navigated through the dimly lit lounge, a dance of proximity that saw their bodies whispering secrets through every incidental graze. His arm brushed against hers, the heat of him seeping into her skin, imprinting on her the map of this journey they were embarking upon.

Behind them, Steven's presence loomed like a silent sentinel. His gaze was a tangible weight upon Dana's back, tracking her every motion with laser precision. There was something acute in the way he observed the interplay between Dana and Richard—the slight catch in her stride, the almost imperceptible pause before she regained her composure. It was a testament to the tempest of emotions she sought to navigate: loyalty and longing locked in a tumultuous embrace.

As they approached the elevator, Dana could feel the ghost of Steven's scrutiny, igniting a war within between the sanctity of the past and the siren call of the present. Richard, ever the conductor of this symphony of tension, managed to mask the electric charge with smooth gestures and an air of casual assurance that seemed to both comfort and compel her.

Yet, despite the calm veneer, Dana's heart beat a frenzied rhythm against her chest—a Morse code of desire that threatened to betray her resolve. She stepped into the elevator, the metallic doors sliding shut with a hush, sealing away the world, leaving her caught in a

The elevator chimed its arrival at the lobby, and as they stepped inside, Dana felt the cool air of the confined space settle around them. She was acutely aware of Steven's silhouette in the background, a silent observer to the unfolding drama. As the doors slid together with a soft whisper, a muted click sealed their ascent from the rest of the world.

Richard stood so close that his warmth radiated against her skin, an almost tangible caress that made her pulse quicken. He was like a flame, and she, the moth irresistibly drawn toward it, even with the potential for devastation looming just behind her shoulder.

"Are you cold, Dana?" Richard's voice was low and husky as he leaned in closer to her.

"A little," she replied, feeling a shiver run down her spine despite the heat radiating from his body.

Without warning, Richard shifted slightly, his hand brushing hers in what seemed like a mere accident. The contact, brief as it was, sent a surge of heat coursing through her veins, setting every nerve ending alight with a hunger she could scarcely comprehend.

"Here, let me help you," he murmured, his breath tickling her ear. "My hands are warm, but not nearly as warm as I want to make you."

Dana's heart skipped a beat at his words, and she couldn't help but feel a flutter of excitement mixed with apprehension. She knew she shouldn't be allowing herself to be drawn towards him like this, but she couldn't resist. It was as if his touch was electric, charging the very air between them with an unspoken promise.

With the brush of his fingers, Dana's heart hammered against her ribs, the rhythm erratic and revealing. She drew in a swift, sharp breath, trying to steady herself, but the air felt too thin, too charged. Her cheeks bloomed with a rosy hue, a silent testament to the tempest within, as Richard's proximity wove an intoxicating spell that left her dizzy with want.

She dared not look at Steven, whose quiet presence she could feel like a shadow across her back. But neither could she tear her gaze away from Richard, whose nearness made her senses reel and her body awaken to a raw and primal yearning.

As the elevator ascended, the pull between them grew, an invisible force that defied reason and threatened to sweep away all her reservations. With each passing floor, Dana felt herself inching closer to a precipice, the drop both terrifying and exhilarating. And all the while, Richard's deliberate caress lingered on her skin, branding her with a desire that knew no bounds.

ii

The subtle shift in the elevator's movement drew Dana's focus back to Richard as he leaned in, his breath a whisper against her ear. "Are you enjoying yourself so far?" His voice, low and seductive, seemed to vibrate through her.

Dana's throat tightened, and she swallowed hard. The simplicity of the question was laced with layers of meaning that sent her thoughts spiraling. She could feel Steven's gaze like a weight upon her, heavy with expectation and silent pleas for fidelity. Her loyalty to him tugged at the edges of her consciousness, an anchor trying to hold fast amidst the storm Richard stirred within her. Yet, amidst the tumult, Richard's allure pulled her in, a siren's song weaving through the defenses she struggled to maintain.

"Yes," she said, though her voice came out softer than she intended, betraying the conflict raging inside her. It was true, in a way—she had never felt more alive, more attuned to every sensation. But it was a dangerous enjoyment, one that danced on the knife-edge of betrayal.

Their eyes met then, locking in a gaze that felt as if it could sear her soul. In Richard's dark eyes, there was an intensity that held her captive, a promise of something more, something forbidden. His pupils were dilated, the blackness enveloping the hazel in a way that mirrored the overwhelming desire she felt—a desire that was now reflected back at her. It was a silent conversation between their gazes, an unspoken acknowledgement of the raw need that pulsed between them.

Dana's breath hitched, and she realized she had been holding it, afraid to break the connection, terrified of where it might lead. Even as her mind screamed at her to look away, to sever the electric thread binding them, her body betrayed her, leaning ever so slightly toward him, like a flower toward the sun. She was caught in his gravitational pull, powerless to escape the orbit of his charisma.

The air in the elevator seemed to grow thicker, charged with the energy of their shared gaze, and Dana knew she was at a turning point. To look away would be to deny the fire that he had kindled within her; to keep looking was to stoke it into an inferno that could consume them both.

The subtle brush of Richard's fingertips against the small of Dana's back was like a spark leaping across dry tinder. A shiver cascaded down her spine, each vertebra lighting up with an almost electric charge that spread through her body in waves. The sensation was more than a mere touch; it was a command that her senses obeyed without question, heightening her desire for him with a tingling urgency that seemed to pulse through her bloodstream.

Dana felt her skin prickle with goosebumps, the fine hairs on her arms standing at attention as if they too were aware of the charged atmosphere Richard was creating around them. She could feel the warmth from his palm seeping through the fabric of her dress, imprinting his touch onto her very being. It was a gentle caress, yet it carried the weight of unspoken promises and unsated longing, leaving her breathless and craving more.

As the elevator continued its silent climb, the closeness of their bodies within the confined space became even more palpable. Richard leaned in, so close that she could feel the heat radiating from his body. He whispered in her ear, each word a velvet caress that sent shivers cascading down her neck and set her nerves alight. His breath was warm against her skin, a stark contrast to the coolness of the metallic walls surrounding them, enveloping her in a cocoon of intimacy.

"I know you crave this," Richard growled, his voice dripping with seductive promises. "Surrender yourself to me and I'll take you on a journey of unbridled pleasures that will leave you trembling and begging for more."

Dana's eyes fluttered closed involuntarily, her body responding with a visceral need to the proximity of his lips. The whisper was barely audible above the hum of the elevator, yet it resonated deep within her, vibrating through her core with an intensity that left her skin tingling with anticipation. Her heart raced, pounding against her ribcage as if desperate to escape or perhaps to beckon Richard even closer.

In that moment, the world outside the elevator ceased to exist. There was only Richard's voice, his touch, the promise of what could be—all conspiring to unravel her resolve and to fan the flames of a desire she had never known could burn so fiercely within her.

iii

The elevator climbed, the numbers on the panel ascending with it, and in that confined space, Dana felt the battle within her rage. Richard's words, each one a spark, had kindled something deep inside her—a fire that threatened to consume her whole. The heat of his proximity was a tangible force, and her mind was awash with images of Steven—his trusting gaze, his gentle smile—and how they contrasted starkly with the smoldering intensity of Richard's dark eyes.

"Kiss Me." Richard's voice broke through her reverie, low and laden with smoldering sensuality.

Richard seemed to sense the inner turmoil plaguing her, his hand shifting from its previous place of comfort on the small of her back. With a daring move, his fingers trailed lower, gliding along the gentle curve of her hip before confidently coming to rest on her thigh. The touch was possessive, claiming her as his own, and it seared through the delicate fabric of her dress to brand her skin beneath. Pulling her closer still, he boldly placed his other hand at the base of her hair, intertwining his fingers in her soft locks and gently pulling her lips to his.

Dana's breath hitched, her body instinctively tensing as her muscles coiled with a blend of excitement and guilt. She felt the weight of Richard's touch like an anchor dragging her further from the safety of her marriage vows. It was a silent demand for her attention, for her surrender, and it ignited a fierce longing that she struggled to suppress.

Their tongues intertwined in a passionate frenzy, eagerly exploring every inch and crevice. The pace quickened as they hungrily devoured each other's mouths, moans and gasps escaping between their feverish kisses. Their bodies pressed together with primal desire, lost in the all-consuming sensation of their heated embrace.

The elevator's quiet motion upwards was relentless, mirroring the ascent of her yearning; each floor passed was a step closer to a precipice from which there would be no return.

iv

The elevator dinged, a gentle but resounding chime that resonated with the pounding of Dana's heart. They had arrived at Richard's floor—a floor that felt like a different universe where the air was thick with the weight of anticipation. As the doors slid open, they stepped out, and Dana could feel the charged space between them crackling with desire. Their bodies were close but not touching, a dance of proximity that set her nerves alight.

As they moved down the plush-carpeted corridor, Richard's hand found hers, his grip firm and insistent. The warmth from his palm seeped into her own, an unspoken promise of what was to come. Dana's mind raced, a whirlwind of trepidation and yearning. She glanced briefly at Richard, whose confident stride never wavered, his every movement exuding a seductive allure that pulled her along in its wake.

With each step toward Richard's hotel room, Dana's loyalty to Steven tugged at her conscience like a child vying for attention amidst the cacophony of an amusement park. It was a relentless pull, yet one that was increasingly overshadowed by the force of her attraction to Richard. The physical connection of their entwined fingers seemed to forge a link straight to her core, where a fierce battle raged between duty and passion. She could almost hear Steven's voice, a distant murmur lost in the tide of her escalating desires.

Dana's breath came in shallow gasps as she wrestled with her emotions, her chest tight with the strain of inner conflict. She wanted to honor the vows she had made, to be the woman who was steadfast and true. But here, in the dimly lit hallway, led by a man who awakened something primal within her, those vows seemed to crumble like ancient ruins—magnificent but eroded by the relentless flow of time and temptation.

Richard stopped before his hotel room door, and the sound of the electronic key card sliding into the slot seemed deafening in the silence. Dana's pulse hammered in her ears, a rhythmic reminder of the precipice upon which she stood—one step into the room might well be a step into an abyss from which there would be no climbing back. And yet, as Richard turned the handle and pushed the door open, her feet moved of their own accord, drawn inexorably into the shadowed sanctuary of the room, and towards an uncertain fate dictated by the untamed yearnings of her heart.

The door creaked open, revealing a dimly lit room that seemed to pulsate with a mixture of anticipation and trepidation. Shadows danced along the walls, casting eerie shapes and playing tricks on Dana's mind. As she peered inside, her heart raced in her chest, each beat a reminder of the dizzying emotions coursing through her veins. Richard's steady hand clasped hers tightly, grounding her as she took in the opulent furnishings and plush velvet curtains that framed a large window overlooking the city skyline. This room held so much promise and danger all at once, and Dana couldn't help but feel both drawn to it and wary of what awaited her within its walls.

She hesitated on the threshold, her mind a tempest of images: Steven's trusting gaze, their shared history, the life they had built together—all pitted against the raw magnetism emanating from Richard, a force that pulled her toward him with the inexorable gravity of a black hole. The air between them crackled with the dangerous electricity of possibilities unexplored, of paths not yet taken.

"Steven," Richard's voice booms with authority. "Please have a seat." He gestures to the chair in front of him, eyes cold and calculating. "It's time for our journey to begin." The weight of those words hangs heavy in the air, signaling a dangerous and uncertain path ahead.

Dana took a breath, trying to steady herself, to find a semblance of clarity through the haze of her desire. But clarity was a distant shore, and she was adrift. With a courage that felt more like recklessness, she stepped across the boundary, surrendering to the unknown. The door closed behind her, shutting out the world with a finality that resonated deep within her bones.

As Richard pulled her into the room, their bodies collided, a collision of flesh and want that sent a shockwave of urgency through her. His touch ignited fires along her skin, and she gasped at the contact, a sound lost in the growing intensity of their proximity. Steven's silhouette was etched into the shadows of her conscience, watching with silent accusation as she allowed herself to be drawn deeper into the fevered embrace of another man.

The door's lock snicked shut, a subtle but definitive sound that seemed to seal her fate. In that moment, time became fluid, and Dana was acutely aware of the precipice upon which they teetered—the brink between restraint and abandon. She could feel Richard's hunger mirroring her own, a tide rising high enough to threaten the levees of her morality.

V

Richard's lips descended upon hers with an intensity that was both alarming and exhilarating. Dana felt a tremor course through her, the touch of his mouth a catalyst that threatened to dissolve the vestiges of her loyalty to Steven. Her mind screamed caution, yet her body betrayed her in its eagerness, pressing into Richard's embrace with a hunger that mirrored his own.

His kiss was a question she dared not answer but found herself responding to regardless. It was as if each brush of his lips chipped away at the resolve that had anchored her to a life she knew, exposing her to the raw tempest of passion swelling within. As his hands found their way to her waist, pulling her closer until there was no space for doubt or reason between them, Dana's heart raced in a dangerous rhythm of desire and trepidation.

The sensation of Richard's fingers tracing the contours of her body seared her skin, igniting a blaze that consumed all thought. The fire spread, a wild thing with a will of its own, melting away her inhibitions like ice beneath a relentless sun. With every touch, Richard mapped her landscape, claiming territory in soft gasps and whispered moans that filled the room with the evidence of her surrender.

As his hands ventured further, exploring the terrain of her curves and edges with a possessive tenderness, Dana found herself adrift in sensations she had never permitted herself to imagine. Each caress was a testament to the yearning that had been lying dormant, now awakened by the deft movements of Richard's hands. Her breaths came in ragged pulls, a silent chorus to the symphony of pleasure that he orchestrated with every deliberate stroke.

The walls she had built, the very essence of her discipline, crumbled beneath the weight of her awakening. In the dimly lit room, with the taste of Richard's kiss still lingering on her lips, Dana felt as though she was shedding an old skin, revealing a part of her that was raw, unexplored, and irrevocably alive.

Dana's breath hitched, hanging in the air like a note held too long. The world narrowed to the feel of Richard's hands roaming with an intensity that threatened to erase all her boundaries. She was acutely aware of every point of contact where his skin met hers, branding her with unspoken promises of ecstasy.

Yet, even as her body arched into his touch, craving more of the intoxicating pleasure he offered, her mind waged a war within the confines of her skull. Images of Steven, her husband—the man she had pledged her life to—flashed before her eyes, their memories a stark contrast against the raw passion she now indulged in with Richard. Each loving smile from Steven, each shared laughter, every quiet moment of companionship, collided with the electric thrill currently coursing through her veins.

A part of her screamed in protest, a desperate plea for reason amidst the tempest of her desire. Loyalty, a value she had held in high esteem, now felt like chains around her heart, pulling her back from the brink of total abandon. The very fabric of her commitment frayed at the edges as Richard's lips traced a feverish path down her neck, igniting a trail of fire that consumed her resolve.

"Steven," she whispered, the name a lifeline thrown into the chaos of her thoughts. It was a whisper drowned out by the sound of her racing heartbeat in her ears, lost in the crescendo of her mounting arousal. Richard's presence enveloped her, an intoxicating force that urged her to forget the world outside this room.

She could feel the struggle within her, the delicate balance between fidelity and want teetering on a knife-edge. Her palms, slick with a mixture of desire and a guilt-laden sweat, pressed against Richard's chest, pushing slightly as if to create a distance she wasn't sure she wanted. There was a fealty to her marriage vows that tugged at her, an anchor in the storm of her emotions, yet it was growing weaker with each second, eroded by the relentless tide of her longing for Richard.

The internal tug-of-war left her gasping, her chest rising and falling in rapid succession. Her mind's eye was filled with visions of Steven's trusting gaze, juxtaposed against the undeniable pull of the man before her, who stoked the once-dormant embers of her passion into a roaring inferno.

In this moment, Dana stood at the precipice, torn between the woman she was with Steven and the one she was becoming with Richard. The two realities clashed violently within her, a maelstrom of love and lust, loyalty and betrayal. With her next breath, she would either step back onto solid ground or leap into the abyss.

CHAPTER 5

Richard's intense gaze locked onto Steven's, a silent challenge burning in the depths of his eyes. Dana stood between them, her breath shallow and her heart racing as she felt the electric tension crackling between the two men.

Richard's voice drips with malice as he leers at her, his eyes dark and calculating. "Now, my dear," he sneers, "let us unveil the secrets hidden beneath this dress." His fingers curl into claws as he reaches for her, ready to tear away the fabric and expose her vulnerability. She shivers in fear, knowing that once revealed, she will be at his mercy.

With expert care, Richard reached out to Dana, his fingers working the buttons of her dress with precision and purpose. Each small click seemed to echo in the charged silence of the room, a precursor to the explosive moment that was about to unfold.

Steven's jaw clenched as he watched, torn between the urge to intervene and the overwhelming force that held him rooted to the spot. He was an outsider in this intimate encounter, yet somehow integral to its power dynamics—a voyeur to the display of dominance playing out before him.

Dana's dress fell open under Richard's skilled touch, revealing her flawless skin and curves encased in delicate lace. His hands moved over her body like a sculptor molding his masterpiece, leaving trails of heat in their wake. The air felt heavy with anticipation as Richard pushed the fabric down until it pooled at Dana's feet.

She stood before them completely exposed, but instead of feeling vulnerable, she felt a sense of exhilaration and submission that sent shivers down her spine.

With each touch, Richard stoked the fire within her, awakening a primal desire that had been dormant for too long. Her body responded eagerly to his commanding yet gentle caresses, a physical testament to the unspoken language that flowed between them.

As they faced Steven, Richard unsnapped Dana's bra with a swift flick of his fingers, revealing her full breasts adorned with rosy peaks of arousal. He traced his hands over them possessively, claiming her as his own in front of their audience. As Steven watched with rapt attention, Richard trailed his fingertips down her stomach to where her lace panties clung tightly to her core. With a single tug, he removed them. The delicate folds of her womanhood glistened with a dewy sheen, like the petals of a rose bathed in morning mist. Each stroke of Richard's fingers sent ripples of pleasure through her, igniting an inferno of desire that consumed her entirely.

"Yes Dana, surrender yourself to me completely." Richard's voice dripped with predatory desire. He hungrily devoured her every move, craving her utter submission. "Let go of all control and give yourself over to my will," he whispered, his eyes gleaming with seductive intent.

Stripped bare and defenseless, she stood before him, her heart thundering in her chest. The overwhelming presence of Richard washed over her like a violent storm, urging her to surrender completely to his dominating will. She was powerless against the pull he held over her, consumed by a desire to submit wholly to him.

In that moment, she belonged to him, body and soul, and she eagerly surrendered to his every touch and command. And as they continued their intimate dance, Steven could only watch in awe and envy of the palpable passion between them.

"Move to the window, my dear," Richard commanded with a commanding tone. "Show the city your true beauty and let it feel the fire burning in your veins with each breath."

Dana obeyed without hesitation, her body trembling with anticipation as she walked towards the massive floor-to-ceiling window, its dark velvet curtains framing her like a work of art. The city lights glittered before her, a perfect contrast to the heat radiating from her flushed skin. She pressed herself against the cool glass, shuddering at the sensation of her hardened nipples grazing its surface, a physical manifestation of her complete submission to Richard's dominance.

"Now, touch yourself my dear," Richard's voice dripped with seduction as he purred, "Unleash the inferno burning inside you and let the city feel the ferocity of your desires."

Dana's trembling hands trailed over her heaving chest, down her quivering stomach, and finally to the slick folds between her legs. The warmth and moisture of her own body greeted her touch, sending shivers of anticipation through her entire being. Her fingers moved with a practiced delicacy, exploring the intricate curves and dips of her womanhood. With each breath, she could feel her desire building, her body responding eagerly to her touch. She closed her eyes and surrendered to the sensations, allowing herself to fully embrace the pleasure coursing through her. The friction from her hot skin against the icy glass sent shivers down her spine as she reveled in the contrast of desire and restraint within her body.

Richard moved silently behind her, his warm breath tickling her ear as he whispered. His hands roamed over her body, sending shivers of anticipation through her. She could feel the desire building within her, a fire that threatened to consume her whole.

"Yes," Richard purred, his voice vibrating against her skin. "Show them who you truly are and who you belong to. Let them bear witness to your wild desires." He pressed soft kisses along the back of her neck and down her shoulders, claiming her in acceptance and igniting a primal heat within her.

As pedestrians walked beneath the towering windows, they need only to turn their gaze upwards to the tantalizing sight above. Bodies, intertwined and flush with excitement, pressed against the frosted glass in a display of raw desire. The curves and shadows cast by the dim lighting only added to the sensual scene, leaving observant passersby spellbound by the erotic scene above them.

ii

Richard guided Dana gently towards the bed, its crisp, white sheets a stark contrast to the heated flush across her skin. With care that belied his earlier assertiveness, he eased her down onto the mattress, her back resting against the cool fabric. His eyes never left hers, an unspoken promise glittering in their depths.

As Richard's hands resumed their exploration, the anticipation seemed to suspend time. He started at her collarbone, fingers tracing the delicate lines of her neck and shoulders. His touch was featherlight, yet every brush of his fingertips sent ripples of excitement through Dana's body. The lightness of his caress was maddening, teasing, promising more with every lingering stroke.

His mouth followed the path set by his hands, lips grazing the sensitive skin of her throat. Soft kisses peppered across her chest, drawing gasps from her lips as his tongue flickered out to taste her. Downward his attention traveled, over the valley between her breasts, circling but never quite touching the pebbled peaks that ached for his mouth.

In the corner of the room, Steven sat motionless, save for the clenching and unclenching of his fists. His gaze was locked on the pair, torn between the desire to look away and the inability to do so. Each kiss, each caress that Richard bestowed upon Dana, struck a chord within him, resonating with a cacophony of jealousy and raw arousal.

Steven's breath hitched, a silent struggle raging within as he watched another man unravel the woman he yearned for.

Meanwhile, Richard continued his meticulous worship of Dana's body. His hands slid down her sides, skimming over the curves of her waist and hips, leaving a trail of fire in their wake. He paused at her thighs, his thumbs brushing the tender skin there, just shy of where she ached for him most. Her breathing grew ragged, a testament to the burgeoning climax that Richard was skillfully, torturously, coaxing from her depths.

Richard's voice boomed with authority as he sternly declared, "You are not allowed to release without my permission. Do you understand?" His eyes narrowed with a fiery intensity, daring his submissive partner to disobey.

She could only nod as her body trembled with a mix of fear and curiosity, unable to defy him knowing that it would likely result in some sort of sexually charged punishment.

Dana's world had narrowed to the feel of Richard's lips and hands, the sound of her own quickening breaths, and the weight of Steven's stare. She was caught in an electrifying limbo, where pleasure teetered on the edge of release. Every touch from Richard was precise, calculated to draw out the intensity of the moment, to stretch her longing into an exquisite agony of need.

Steven could see it—the way her body arched toward Richard, seeking more, the way her hands fisted the sheets in a silent plea. It was an image both beautiful and tormenting, and it seared itself into his memory, a visceral reminder of the passion and power at play before him.

Richard's movements were unhurried, deliberate, as he released himself from the constraints of his clothing. Piece by piece, the fabric fell away, revealing the man in all his raw masculinity. He stood over Dana, a statue carved from desire. His erection stood tall and proud, a symbol of his desire and arousal. It was long and thick, veins pulsing with every beat of his heart. The head glinted in the dim light, glistening with a sheen of his passion.

Dana lay beneath him, her chest rising and falling with an increasing tempo, a reflection of the anticipation that thrummed through her veins. As Richard towered above her, a looming presence of power and carnal intent, she could feel the air between them crackle, charged with the promise of fulfillment.

His knees dipped the bed as he leaned over her, his shadow engulfing her form in a warm darkness. Then, his breath caressed her ear, the heat of it sending a shiver down her spine. His voice, when it came, was a low rumble against the shell of her ear, each syllable laced with authority and a gentleness that belied the fervor in his eyes.

"Are you prepared for the ecstasy that awaits, Dana?" His voice was a seductive caress against her trembling nerves. "Put your faith in me, and I will guide you to new heights of pleasure, beyond anything you've ever experienced."

The resonance of his voice vibrated through her, a soothing command that coaxed her breaths to quicken further, her body preparing for the union it craved. In his words, she found strength and solace, a beacon guiding her through the tumultuous sea of her own desire.

Already lost in the maze of sensation Richard had orchestrated, Dana clung to his assurance, allowing herself to be swept away by the tide of passion that threatened to break over her. With every word he spoke, Richard claimed a little more of her, his presence a steady force in the tempest of her arousal.

iii

Richard's touch descended, a slow and deliberate journey from the curve of Dana's waist to the roundness of her hips. His palms were both firm and exploratory, tracing the rise and dip of her flesh with an artist's precision. Her skin hummed beneath his fingers, a silent song of yearning that resonated deep within her core.

She felt her hips canting towards him, a wordless plea for more. The fire he kindled spread, licking along her thighs with each sweep of his hands. It was as if he mapped every inch of her, charting territories she herself had barely acknowledged. The heat pooled, an ember in her veins set aflame by Richard's meticulous attention.

Dana's body sang with newfound sensitivity; every touch was a note played on the strings of her desire. She marveled at how effortlessly he coaxed her arousal to the fore, a crescendo of sensation that made her want to arch into his every caress. She was clay under his ministrations, molding to his will, her very essence reshaped by the hunger he invoked.

He lingered where thigh met hip, a teasing pressure that promised so much yet withheld the culmination she craved. Dana's breath hitched, caught in the tangle of anticipation and need. With each expert touch, Richard drew her closer to the brink, to that precipice of ecstasy she ached to tumble over, her body a testament to the potency of his mastery.

Richard's fingers, now audacious and unrelenting, delved into the silken folds of Dana's desire. He explored her with a relentless curiosity, his touch dancing over her most intimate areas like a musician playing an instrument only he could master. With each stroke and swirl, he painted strokes of pleasure on the canvas of her flesh, each one more daring than the last.

Dana's moans punctuated the silence of the room, each one a chorus that celebrated the sensations Richard elicited from deep within her. She twisted beneath him, hips rising in silent supplication, inviting him to venture deeper, to claim her completely. Her hands clutched at the sheets, balling the soft fabric in her grasp as Richard's fingers continued their exquisite torment.

The tension within her coiled tighter, a spring wound to its limit. The world narrowed to the point of Richard's touch, everything else fading into oblivion. She was acutely aware of every movement, every deliberate caress that brought her closer to the edge.

Richard's hands glided over Dana's smooth skin, caressing every inch of her body with a gentle yet firm touch. With skilled precision, he spread open her soft folds, exposing her eager flesh to his hungry gaze. His tongue danced along her sensitive spots, igniting sparks of pleasure that rippled through her entire being. Dana's back arched off the bed, the sensations coursing through her body overwhelming her senses. She could feel herself teetering on the edge of an orgasm, desperate for release as Richard continued to drive her closer and closer to the edge.

The only word Dana could manage to choke out was a desperate "please." But Richard showed no mercy, rising ever so slightly from between her quivering legs. A sinister grin crept across his face as he whispered, "Not yet, my dear. We have much further to go on this journey." She whimpered in fear and anticipation, knowing there was no escape from the intensity of his desires.

He focused his attention on her most sensitive spot, flicking it with fervent strokes of his tongue that sent electric shocks of pleasure through her whole body. Dana cried out in pure ecstasy, unable to contain the pleasure that was consuming her.

Richard's skilled hands ignited a wildfire of pleasure within her, each fierce sensation consuming her with a relentless intensity. She writhed beneath him, unable to control the powerful currents surging through her body as he drove her towards a climax she had never known before - an all-encompassing peak that shattered every sense and left her gasping for more.

With a guttural moan, Dana tumbled over that edge, exploding into a million pieces as ecstasy claimed every inch of her being. She shattered under Richard's touch, spiraling into a mind-numbing climax that left her breathless.

Richard's hands, which had been eagerly exploring her body, suddenly ceased their movements. His commanding voice cut through the air, halting any further pleasure she may have been experiencing.

"Oh no my dear," he said firmly, his tone filled with disapproval. "You did not have permission for that release." A pause followed as he contemplated her mistake. "I'm afraid some compensation must be paid for this transgression."

His words hung in the air, ominous and foreboding. She could only imagine what kind of punishment he had in mind for her disobedience. Her heart raced with fear and anticipation, knowing she would do anything to please him, even if it meant facing consequences for her actions.

iv

With a commanding tone, Richard barked, "Stand up." Dana's heart raced as she rose gingerly from the bed, still shaking off the effects from her recent release. She stepped towards him, her feet sinking into the plush carpet.

"Now, on your knees," he commanded. "Lift your chin and open your mouth."

At his instruction, Dana dropped to her knees at the foot of the bed, looking up at him with a mix of nervousness and anticipation. His intense gaze roamed over her exposed body, taking in every inch of her with a hunger that made her pulse quicken.

He reached out to run a hand through her hair before gripping it tightly and pulling her head back slightly. "You disobeyed me," he said sternly. "Do you understand why that was wrong?"

Dana nodded, feeling a mixture of guilt and desire wash over her. She knew she should have waited for his permission before allowing herself to climax.

"I'm going to have to teach you a lesson," Richard continued. "Do you trust me?"

Dana hesitated for a moment before replying with a shaky voice, "Yes."

Richard's lips curled into a mischievous grin as he leaned down to retrieve his coiled belt from its perch on the dresser. He unfolded it with a flick of his wrist, making it snap loudly. Dana watched with a mix of excitement and fear as he positioned himself in front of her, the belt coiled in his hand like a serpent ready to strike.

"Open your mouth wider," he instructed, his voice low and commanding.

With trembling hands, Dana obeyed, feeling her heart race with anticipation. She braced herself for the impact of the leather against her skin, but instead, Richard ran it teasingly across her lips and tongue before slowly running it over her shoulders and down her back. He roughly grabbed her hands and encircled the belt around them buckling it tight behind her.

She watched him with wide eyes as he stepped closer, his hard length inches from her face.

"Take it in," he commanded, his voice hoarse with desire.

Dana leaned forward and took him into her mouth, slowly sliding her lips over him until she reached the base. She could feel his hand tighten in her hair as she bobbed her head up and down, trying to remember everything she had seen in steamy movies.

Richard groaned above her, encouraging her to continue. Her own body responded to his pleasure, feeling arousal pooling between her legs.

"That's it," he praised. "You're doing so well."

With each thrust of Richard's hips and every moan that escaped his lips, Dana felt herself growing more confident and eager to please him.

Suddenly, Richard pulled away from her with a sharp intake of breath. Dana looked up at him with confusion as he reached out to pull her to her feet.

Richard sat down on the edge of the bed and with a hard grip on Dana's hair, he forcefully pulled her across his lap, her body trembling with fear as she felt the cold metal of the belt biting into her wrists. As if in slow motion, she bent over obediently, offering up her vulnerable backside to Steven's piercing stare from the corner. The room was filled with an oppressive silence, broken only by the sound of Dana's shallow breaths and the looming threat of Richard's wrath. With every second that passed, she could feel her punishment drawing closer and closer. Dana's mouth went dry with nervousness as she tasted the metallic tang of adrenaline in her mouth.

"You were given explicit instructions, yet you chose to defy them. Do you understand the gravity of your actions, my dear?"

Dana's head nods frantically as she chokes out a shaky "yes". Richard glared down at her; his dark eyes filled with a predatory gleam as he sat on the edge of the bed. A sadistic smile played on his lips as he gazed at Dana, his willing captive. "To earn your release, you must first endure the pain and longing that precedes it," he murmured, sending shivers down her spine. His fingers traced a tantalizing path down her trembling body until they reached her thighs, where he circled her sensitive clit slowly and deliberately, eliciting moans from her parted lips. "This pleasure you feel now will be met with equal parts agony," he whispered huskily in her ear. And with one swift motion, his other hand came crashing down on Dana's bare ass, leaving behind a searing red welt and a stinging sensation that only fueled her desire for escape. Every nerve in her body jolted with conflicting sensations of pain and pleasure, driving her closer to the brink of ecstasy.

Dana's mind was a blur as Richard continued his punishment, alternating between pleasure and pain. She couldn't help but let out a low moan with each strike, her body craving more of the intense sensations. Her hands clawed at the belt tightly, her nails digging into the hard leather as she struggled to hold back her cries.

Steven watched from his spot in the corner, his eyes darkening with desire and admiration for Richard's control over Dana. He could see the pleasure etched on Dana's face, even through the mask of pain she was experiencing. He could also sense her growing need for release, just as he himself felt a primal urge to jump in and take control.

Richard's hand moved from her clit to her wet folds, teasing her entrance with his fingers before plunging them deep inside. Dana let out a loud gasp at the sudden intrusion, arching her back in response. With each thrust of his fingers, she could feel herself getting closer and closer to the edge.

But just as she was about to tip over into an intense orgasm, Richard abruptly stopped. Dana let out a frustrated groan at being denied once again. But before she could voice her protest, Richard whispered in her ear, "Not yet my dear."

v

Richard pulled away from her completely and stood up from the bed.

Dana collapses onto the floor before him, her body trembling and gasping for air as waves of pleasure and pain course through her. The intensity of Richard's sadistic demeanor softens into a tender, almost loving expression, his eyes glinting with a devilish playfulness. "Now, my dear," he says in a low whisper, "it's time for you to experience true surrender." With skilled hands, he pulls Dana towards him and releases her from the tight grip of the belt. Laying her gently onto the cool sheets of the bed, he looms over her with a commanding presence that sends shivers down her spine. She can't help but feel both anxious and eagerly anticipating what comes next from this dark and alluring man, wondering what new heights of pleasure and pain he will bring her to.

Her lungs nearly burst from the forceful gasp as his powerful hands seized her thighs, dragging her towards the edge of the bed. His touch was electrifying and forceful, sparking a wildfire of anticipation that roared through her body. The heat radiating from his skin enveloped her, drawing her in closer as he pressed against her with a primal hunger.

Richard's lust consumed him, driving him to thrust into her with a primal force that left them both gasping for air. Their bodies collided, igniting an inferno of need and desire that coursed through every nerve and sinew. As he plunged his throbbing manhood deep inside her, she was overcome with a wave of indescribable pleasure. A symphony of primal sounds erupted from their lips as they surrendered to the raw, carnal fire consuming them. In perfect synchronization, their bodies moved in a frenzied dance of passion and ecstasy, lost in the all-encompassing intensity of their desire for each other.

Dana's back arched off the bed as he claimed her with every forceful thrust. He moved with a controlled aggression, each movement igniting a new wave of pleasure and sending her heart racing. She was completely at his mercy, surrendering herself to the unspoken promise of his powerful body.

For Dana, time lost all meaning as Richard's body merged with hers in a dance of passion and desire. The room was filled with the sounds of their lovemaking, the rhythmic slapping of skin on skin echoing off the walls.

Richard's hands roamed over her body, mapping every inch of her with a possessiveness that made her feel cherished. She surrendered to him completely, allowing herself to be swept away by the intensity of their connection.

With raw strength and primal desire, he maneuvered her body into positions that allowed him to penetrate even deeper. Richard's movements became more urgent, his pace quickening as he thrust into Dana with a hunger that belied his control. She could feel the intensity building between them, their bodies moving in perfect sync as they sought the ultimate release.

Dana's nails dug into Richard's back, her legs wrapping tightly around him as she met his every thrust with equal fervor. She was lost in the sensation of his body against hers, consumed by the all-consuming pleasure that he brought her.

Their lovemaking reached a fever pitch, their bodies tangled together in a fierce and unrelenting battle for dominance. Richard growled low in his throat, his grip on her tightening as he claimed her with each powerful thrust.

The sound of their bodies slapping together echoed through the room, mingling with their gasps and moans of pleasure. Dana felt like she was flying, carried away on a wave of passion that threatened to consume her completely.

With a fierce intensity, he flipped her onto her stomach, his strong hands gripping her hips and guiding her body as he plunged into her with raw, primal force. Each thrust sent bolts of lightning through her veins, igniting a fire deep within as their bodies moved in sync, creating a symphony of passion and desire. She surrendered to the overwhelming sensations, lost in the heat of their untamed connection.

His towering figure loomed over her, dominating the space with his commanding presence. He seized her hair in a tight grip, pulling and growling in her ear, "Look at me."

She complied, locking eyes with him as he plunged into her with unrelenting force. With each powerful thrust, their bodies collided in a wild frenzy, her breasts bouncing and swaying in rhythm to his movements, sending waves of pleasure through them both.

Their erotic dance echoed throughout the room, the wet sounds of their bodies colliding and her mewls of satisfaction filling the air. His deep grunts mixed with her high-pitched cries as he continued to dominate her body. She reveled in his strength and control, surrendering herself completely to him in this moment of pure ecstasy.

His hands, rough and commanding, guided her limbs with a firm grip as he thrust into her with unrelenting force. Every movement was a bold declaration of possession, sending waves of intense pleasure through her body and igniting primal urges she never knew existed.

Dana's mind was consumed by pure sensation, every nerve ending alight as she lost herself in the pleasure that Richard brought to her. She felt like she was floating on a cloud of ecstasy, held up only by the strength of their mutual desire.

Their bodies moved together in perfect synchrony, each movement bringing them closer and closer to another climax. Sweat glistened on their skin as they perspired from the intensity of their lovemaking.

The pressure within Dana built once again as Richard's thrusts became more urgent. She could feel him pulsing inside her, driving them both towards another explosive release.

Richard's voice dripped with malice as he gripped her trembling arms. "Now my dear," he hissed, eyes blazing with sadistic glee, "it is time for you to understand the true purpose of this journey."

With one final, powerful thrust, their bodies pressed together in a frenzy of passion. Richard's essence exploded inside her, igniting every nerve ending and causing her to shatter into oblivion as a wave of pleasure washed over them both. A symphony of moans and gasps filled the room as they rode out their orgasms in perfect harmony, each sensation amplified by the other's touch. In that moment, there was nothing but pure bliss, the outside world faded away as they were consumed by their shared ecstasy.

As they lay tangled together in the aftermath, Dana felt complete contentment wash over her. She had never experienced anything like this before.

vi

Steven's hands clenched into fists, the fabric of the armchair biting into his palms. He watched, a silent spectator to the tempestuous sea of passion that unfolded before him. His breath hitched in his throat as Richard's rhythmic dominance over Dana reached its crescendo, her cries of ecstasy a piercing melody that resonated with Steven's darkest desires.

The jealousy that gnawed at Steven's insides was a fierce, living thing, clawing its way through his gut with every moan that escaped Dana's lips. Yet, paradoxically, it was entwined with an undeniable arousal, a heat that coursed through his veins and pooled heavily in his loins.

He was torn, caught between the primal urge to claim and the burning pleasure of witnessing Dana's surrender. The two emotions twisted within him, a chaotic dance that left him breathless and on edge, his body aching for release but his heart shackled by the complexity of his feelings.

As the waves of Dana's orgasm slowly receded, Richard's movements stilled. He lowered his sweat-glistened body onto hers, enveloping her in an embrace that spoke of more than just physical satisfaction. His broad chest heaved against her back, and his voice, tender and low, murmured words of comfort into the shell of her ear.

Richard's arms wrapped around Dana, his fingers tracing soothing patterns across her flushed skin as she gasped softly, coming back to herself from the heights of her climactic flight. In this quiet afterglow, their connection seemed to weave itself into something deeper, threads of emotion binding them together in a tapestry rich with color and warmth.

Steven could only watch as Richard held her close, the raw intensity of their intimacy a stark contrast to the relentless storm of passion that had raged mere moments ago. As he observed their gentle communion, the knots of conflict in Steven's chest began to loosen, giving way to a reluctant admiration for the profound bond that had formed before his eyes, a bond that both pained and intrigued him in equal measure.

He remained still, the tumult within him subsiding into a silent contemplation of the scene before him, the intimate tableau of Dana and Richard speaking volumes in the hush that followed their fervent coupling.

In the charged silence, Dana lay still, her breaths now soft whispers against Richard's neck. His arms remained her shelter, his presence an anchor in the sea of tumultuous emotions that had just swept over them. She could feel the weight of Steven's gaze upon them, heavy with things unsaid, his eyes a mirror to the complexity of feelings she herself was trying to understand.

Richard shifted slightly, loosening his hold but not withdrawing completely. He propped himself up on one elbow to look down at Dana, his eyes searching hers for any sign of regret or discomfort. What he found instead was a silent question—a wonder at what they had just shared and where it might lead.

"Are you alright?" His voice, though low, cut through the stillness like a lifeline thrown across the waters of uncertainty.

Dana nodded, her lips curving into a small, genuine smile. "Yes," she murmured, the word barely more than a breath yet holding the weight of her complex emotions—satisfaction mingled with a hint of apprehension for the unknown future.

Meanwhile, Steven sat motionless, the inner turmoil of arousal and jealousy now giving way to a quiet introspection. The raw display of dominance and submission had awakened a deep-seated longing within him, a desire to possess and be possessed with such intensity. Yet, as he watched Richard's tender care for Dana, he couldn't help but feel an unfamiliar ache—the sting of exclusion from the profound connection they shared.

With a subtle shift is his seat, Steven acknowledged the longing within him, letting the tight coil of his jealousy unravel just enough to make room for a different kind of yearning—one that sought understanding and perhaps even participation in this intricate dance of desire.

The room, though silent, spoke volumes as each of them navigated the delicate aftermath. Their desires, once a confluence of raging torrents, settled into quieter streams, each following its own course yet inevitably drawn to the others. It was a silent pact, unspoken yet understood, that what had transpired here would forever change the dynamics of their relationship.

CHAPTER 6

Richard's lips, warm and insistent, pressed against Dana's for a fleeting moment that seemed to capture the essence of the evening. It was a kiss imbued with gratitude and farewell, a sealing of the shared pleasures they had indulged in. As he pulled back, the cool air of the room rushed between them, a stark contrast to the heat that had just been.

"Thank you," Richard murmured, his voice laced with a resonant sincerity as he stood from the bed, his movements fluid and assured. He glanced at both Dana and Steven, his eyes reflecting a genuine appreciation. "Tonight was truly wonderful."

Dana watched, her chest rising and falling with each breath, as Richard began to clothe himself. The fabric of his shirt slipped over toned muscles, a subtle reminder of how they had danced under his skin only moments ago. He was careful to maintain an air of elegance even in such mundane actions, the mark of a man who understood the art of leaving as much as entering.

"Please...keep the room for as long as you like. And should you ever want to..." His words trailed off, but the implication hung in the air, lingering like the scent of their intertwined desires. "I am at your service." With a final nod and a smile that spoke of secrets only they would share, Richard turned towards the door, exiting their temporary sanctuary with a soft click that resounded in the silent aftermath of his departure.

The room felt expansive now, the absence of Richard casting a palpable void. Dana shifted, her bare skin grazing the crisp sheets as she pivoted to face Steven. He joined her on the edge of the bed, side by side—their proximity a testament to what had transpired. Their bodies still hummed, echoing touches that were both foreign and intimately familiar.

Steven's presence next to her was grounding, his body exuding a warmth that beckoned her closer even without touch. He was her constant, her anchor in the sea of passion they had navigated together. In the dim light, she could see the sheen of sweat on his brow, remnants of the feverish excitement that had gripped them both.

They shared the silence, letting it wrap around them like a shroud, comforting in its own right. It was a silence filled with unspoken words and the reverberation of their racing hearts. The encounter with Richard had been a tempest, a whirlwind that had swept through their lives, leaving them more exposed, yet somehow more whole than before.

Their intertwined experiences with Richard lingered, a shared memory etched into their private history. And as they sat there, the echoes of their tryst played across their senses, a symphony of carnal discovery that promised to haunt and invigorate them for time untold.

ii

Steven's fingers traced an invisible line across the expanse of rumpled sheets between them before finally finding Dana's hand. She felt the weight of his touch, a subtle pressure that spoke volumes, conveying ownership and comfort all at once. His skin was warm against hers, a contrast to the cool aftermath of their shared passions.

In the silence, Dana turned her palm upward, interlocking her fingers with his. The gesture was simple yet intimate, reinforcing the bond that thrummed with life beneath the surface. Steven's thumb caressed the back of her hand in rhythmic motions, a wordless symphony that soothed the riot of sensations within her.

Lifting her gaze, Dana sought out Steven's eyes, those twin pools of emotion that had always seemed to reflect his soul. Her breath caught slightly as she navigated the complexities there, the intricate dance of feelings he didn't need to voice. There were shadows, yes—fleeting ghosts of uncertainty—but it was the luminous glow of love that shone brightest, casting away any lingering darkness.

In that look, in the unguarded moment they shared, Dana found an affirmation more powerful than any words could convey. It was there in the steadfast hold of his gaze, the tender fortress he had built around her with just his eyes. Love, fierce and unwavering, anchored her to him, to this new realm of their existence they had bravely charted together.

Steven's chest rose and fell with a steadiness that belied the churn of emotions Dana could sense simmering beneath his calm exterior. He cleared his throat softly, a prelude to breaking the silence that had wrapped around them like a cocoon.

"Thank you," he began, his voice carrying the weight of his vulnerability like an offering. "For... embracing this with me." His fingers squeezed hers ever so slightly, their entwined hands a testament to the odyssey they had embarked upon together. "Exploring my desire, our desires, it's... I think it's deepened what we have. More than I could've imagined. Do you feel the same?"

Dana watched the words shape themselves on Steven's lips, each one infused with raw gratitude. The earnest timber of his voice resonated within her, touching parts of her soul reserved only for the most intimate of confessions. She nodded, the movement small but significant, as myriad emotions tumbled through her own being.

"I... I've felt so much," she admitted, her voice a whisper that seemed too loud in the stillness of the room. Her eyes, wide and unshielded, sought his. "Jealousy, yes, guilt, and arousal that surprised even me. But there's also this..." She paused, searching for the words that could encapsulate the maelstrom within. "... this liberation, this self-discovery that I didn't expect."

Her confession hung between them, a fragile truth that connected them even more deeply, a shared secret that was theirs alone to understand. They were voyagers charting unknown territories, learning the contours of each other's hearts anew.

Steven's eyes held a steady light, the kind that comes from a man who has seen the edge of his own limits and found them worthy. He listened, truly listened, as Dana's chest rose and fell with the tide of emotions still washing over her from the evening's revelations.

"Richard..." she began, her voice steadier than she expected. Her eyes dropped to where their hands met, to the physical proof that Steven was with her, not just in body, but soul-deep. She raised her gaze to meet his once more. "His touch was like fire, igniting something raw within me. Something primal." Her voice dropped to a whisper, yet every word vibrated with intensity. "He awakened desires I never knew lay dormant. And you, Steven, you gave me the freedom to explore those shadowed corners of my passion."

Steven's expression didn't falter; he absorbed her words, the undercurrents of her newfound yearning. In that moment, they stood on sacred ground, a place where vulnerability and desire intertwined, where the echoes of their exploration rang with the promise of deeper connection.

iii

Steven's fingers curled around Dana's with a firmness that had her pulse quickening. The subtle pressure spoke volumes, echoing the possessiveness that flashed in his eyes—a silent claim that tethered her to him amidst the sea of emotions swirling within them both. His voice, when it broke through the charged silence, carried the weight of confession. "Dana," he said, his tone threaded with complexities, "there's a part of me that wrestles with jealousy—to see you touched by another." He paused, his thumb caressing the back of her hand in an assuring rhythm. "Yet, there's this undeniable arousal, and more than that—an overwhelming pride. To witness you delve into your desires without restraint... it's profound."

The raw honesty in Steven's admission bridged the space between them, pulling Dana closer. Her breath mingled with his as she angled her body toward his warmth, their skin barely grazing. She studied the depth of his gaze, finding solace in the familiar storm of green before whispering her truth. "Steven, my love," she began, her voice a silken thread weaving gratitude into the tapestry of their shared history. "Thank you for being the strength behind my surrender, for craving the sight of my pleasure through another's hands and not judging me for how I reacted, for what I gave to him."

In the closeness of their near embrace, they found a sanctuary, a silent vow renewing itself in the space where their breaths intertwined.

Steven's fingertips grazed Dana's cheek, a whisper-soft touch that drew her eyes to his. Delicately, he tucked a rebellious strand of hair behind her ear, the intimacy of the gesture speaking volumes more than words ever could. "Dana," he murmured, the tender cadence of his voice wrapping around her like a comforting shroud, "seeing you in the throes of such pleasure tonight—it did something to me. Something deep and unshakeable. It only amplified the love I hold for you, reinforcing every trust, every thread that binds us."

In the quivering silence that stretched between them, Dana felt a smile tug at the corners of her mouth. The turmoil of emotions that had danced through her during their encounter began to settle, leaving behind a profound sense of peace. She reached up, her hand covering his, pressing his palm against her cheek. "Steven," she breathed out, the name a talisman against any lingering doubts. "I've never felt more alive, more connected to my own being—and to you. This exploration... it's ignited a passion within me, a self-discovery that I owe to your love and strength. I'm grateful, so deeply grateful for everything we are together."

In the soft glow of the hotel room, with the outside world held at bay, they were cocooned in their shared vulnerability and the raw honesty of their connection. Their journey had taken them to realms neither one had charted before, and yet, as they sat together on the precipice of this new frontier, they found themselves anchored firmly in each other's hearts.

iv

Steven's arms enveloped Dana, drawing her close until no space remained between them. His embrace was a fortress, his heartbeat a drum echoing her own. They fit together, two halves of a whole that the night had forged anew. She felt his muscles, still tense with unsaid emotions, relax as they melded into one entity.

Their lips met in a kiss that was both a seal on the evening's revelations and a promise for the future. It was deep and consuming, a passionate dance where their tongues played the rhythm of their shared pulse. The taste of him was familiar yet charged with the electric thrill of the unexplored paths they had just begun to tread.

The kiss broke, but the space it left was filled with something even more intense. Their eyes locked—a mirror of souls laid bare, reflecting the tumultuous odyssey they'd embarked upon. In Steven's gaze, Dana found a kaleidoscope of desire, fear, admiration, and an unwavering resolve that matched her own.

They were silent, words unnecessary in the face of such profound understanding. This journey, with its delicate interplay of trust and vulnerability, had only just begun. Yet as they peered into the depth of each other's eyes, there was an unspoken agreement that whatever lay ahead, they would face it together, eager to explore every shade and nuance of the desires that bound them.

Gently, Steven guided Dana down onto the silk sheets, their bodies sliding into a familiar embrace. The bed accepted their weight with a soft sigh, as if it too recognized the sanctity of this moment. There was no urgency in their movements—only the slow rhythm of two hearts learning a deeper beat.

Dana felt the brush of Steven's fingertips tracing the contours of her collarbone, a silent ode to the valleys and peaks that had become his to explore. She reciprocated with equal reverence, her hands gliding over the contours of his back, muscles yielding beneath her touch. Their entwined limbs spoke a language older than words, each caress a stanza in the poem they composed together.

As Steven's lips found the hollow at the base of her throat, a shiver of anticipation danced along Dana's skin. The warmth of his breath against her exposed flesh was both a soothing balm and a spark of desire; it calmed any lingering uncertainties and ignited a passion reborn from their shared exploration.

The world beyond their cocoon seemed to fade into obscurity, leaving only the purity of connection between them. With each movement, they wove an intricate tapestry of trust and intimacy, their bodies moving in perfect harmony. Every shift, every sigh was a brushstroke on the canvas of night, splashing it with vibrant colors that reflected the depth of their love. This was more than just physical pleasure; it was an intimate masterpiece that they were creating together. And as they lost themselves in the moment, time seemed to stand still, captured within the confines of their own little world.

v

In a primal act of possession, Steven plunged inside Dana, filling every inch of her and reclaiming her as his own. The remnants of Richard's touch vanished, replaced by Steven's steadfast presence. As they merged as one once again, their bodies writhed in unison, consumed by a primal need for each other.

Their movements became more urgent, each seeking to claim the other's pleasure as their own. With every thrust, Dana felt herself unraveling into a state of pure ecstasy. Steven's hands roamed over her body with a hunger that matched her own; his touch igniting flames that spread throughout her being.

As she reached the peak of pleasure, Dana cried out Steven's name, her body convulsing around him. In that moment, she felt complete and whole once again, as if all the broken pieces inside her had finally been healed.

But even in the throes of passion, there was a tenderness between them that transcended mere physical pleasure. In each other's arms, they found solace and understanding; two souls entwined in an unbreakable bond.

As they lay entangled in the aftermath of their lovemaking, Dana traced circles on Steven's chest with her fingertips. She could feel his heart beating steadily beneath her palm and it served as a reminder that this was real; their love was real.

Steven turned to face her with a soft smile on his lips. "I love you," he said simply but sincerely.

Tears pricked at Dana's eyes at those three little words. They held so much weight and yet were so effortless for him to say. In them, she heard all the emotions that had gone unspoken between them for too long: his fear of losing her to Richard, his admiration for her strength and resilience, and above all else, his undying love for her.

"I love you too," Dana whispered, her voice trembling with emotion

As sleep began to claim them, their fingers remained entwined, a tangible reminder of their interdependence. With the final flicker of consciousness, Dana felt the promise of dawn within her. Together, they drifted into slumber, the next chapter of their journey awaiting in the realm of dreams, ready to be written with the ink of their continued passion.

CHAPTER 7.

The morning light streamed through the half-drawn curtains, casting a warm glow on Dana's skin as she stepped across the threshold of their home. The door closed with a soft click behind them, and for a moment, it was as if the world outside ceased to exist. Her senses were still alight, every nerve ending humming with the vivid memories from the night spent in Richard's enigmatic presence.

Steven, ever the grounding force in her life, turned to her with that familiar glint in his eye that spoke volumes of his love and the pride he felt. Without a word, he reached out, his fingers brushing against hers—a touch that promised safety and understanding. It was the same hand that had guided her through their exploration of shadowed desires, the same hand that now anchored her to this new reality they had woven together.

Dana let her hand slip into Steven's, feeling the roughness of his palm—a stark contrast to the tender way he handled her heart. He led her, step by step, through the quiet hall adorned with pictures of their shared life, echoing with silent laughter and whispers of intimacy past. There was a new chapter being written in their journey, one that crackled with the electricity of the previous night's revelations.

The living room was awash with the comfort of familiarity, the plush couch standing as an island of solace amidst a sea of emotions. Steven gestured towards it, his eyes never leaving hers, inviting her to sink into its cushioned embrace. With each step, the fabric of her clothes seemed to whisper across her sensitized skin, a gentle reminder of hands that had roamed with purpose and pleasure.

As Dana settled into the couch, the oversized cushions enveloping her form, she glanced up at Steven. His presence was a balm to the whirlwind that danced within her. There was no need for words just yet; their connection transcended speech, communicated through the intertwining of fingers and the shared warmth of bodies that had discovered new horizons together.

The world outside the expansive window seemed to slow its pace, the gentle dance of leaves in the morning breeze mirroring the tranquil stillness that filled the room. Dana and Steven sat side by side, the weight of their bodies sinking into the soft fabric of the couch, forming an island of repose in the quiet space.

They exchanged a silent language through locked gazes, no words necessary to articulate the profound shift that had occurred within them both. The air hummed with the vivid recollection of the night before, each pulse beat a resonant echo of shared pleasure and exploration.

Steven's chest rose and fell with a rhythm that spoke of deep contentment, his eyes reflecting the myriad emotions that danced within Dana's own. He reached out, his hand brushing hers with deliberate gentleness—a touch that sought to affirm their unspoken bond.

The moment stretched, infinite and intimate, until finally, Steven broke the silence. His voice, warm and soft as velvet, carried an undercurrent of awe. "Dana," he began, the timbre of his words wrapping around her like a comforting shroud, "I am so incredibly proud of you."

She turned slightly towards him, drawn by the sincerity that suffused his every syllable. Steven's gaze was unwavering, his expression open and vulnerable in a way that invited absolute trust.

"Last night," he continued, his fingers tracing an idle path along the back of her hand, "you embraced your desires with such courage, exploring depths within yourself with grace and honesty." Each word was a tender caress, recognizing the strength it had taken for her to reveal the facets of her submissive side. "Your willingness to explore, it means more than I can say." In his voice, there was a note of reverence, a testament to the sacred ground they had tread together in the realm of their deepest fantasies.

Dana felt something within her unfurl at his accolade, her heart expanding with the love and respect that flowed so freely between them. Steven's affirmation was a gift, one that acknowledged her journey and the mutual devotion that fueled their continuous exploration of passion and intimacy.

A flush of warmth spread across Dana's face as she looked into Steven's eyes. The intensity of their shared experience still echoed in the quiet of the room, reverberating through her being. She reached for his hand, her voice a hushed whisper tinged with gratitude.

"Steven," she said, her voice barely above the softest sigh, "your support, your love, without you, I could never have journeyed so far, so deep within myself."

Her words hung in the air, delicate and sincere. There was a tremor of emotion that belied the usual confidence she carried. This vulnerability, this open gratitude, was a rare gem offered only to him.

Steven's response was not with words but with the proximity of his presence. He leaned towards her, the closeness of his body exuding a comforting warmth. His lips found the shell of her ear, and he whispered, each word a silken thread weaving a tapestry of adoration.

"May brave and beautiful Dana," his breath caressed her skin, sending shivers down her spine. "Your willingness to be vulnerable, letting go and trusting in us, in our love —it's awe-inspiring."

She closed her eyes for a moment, savoring the sensation of his lips so close, the sound of his voice wrapping around her like an intimate embrace. It was more than the physical connection they shared; it was the emotional bond, unbreakable and profound, that enveloped her now.

ii

Dana drew in a deep breath, the fabric of her shirt fluttering against her chest as her heart swelled within. The air was thick with a sense of contentment that seemed to stretch and fill every corner of the room. Her body still hummed, a symphony of tingles playing over her skin, each note a reminder of the pleasures that had unfolded—a melody of sensation that Richard's touch had composed upon her flesh, now echoing in the tranquility of their home.

Steven reached for her hand, his fingers grazing hers before intertwining tightly. The simple act resonated with profound intimacy; a silent language spoken fluently between their entwined palms. As they locked gazes, something passed between them—an understanding that words could never fully capture. It was more than acknowledgment; it was an affirmation of the journey they'd taken together, the barriers they'd broken, and the trust they'd fortified.

Their hands lay joined, a testament to the unity of their desires and the harmony of their souls. Each point where their skin met seemed to pulse with shared history and mutual anticipation for the future. In this quiet connection, Dana found a peace that was both grounding and liberating, an anchor in Steven's steadfast love and a sail catching the winds of newfound freedom.

Steven's hand lifted, a whisper of movement in the stillness of the living room. His fingertips brushed against Dana's cheek, a touch as light as a petal drifting on a summer breeze. His eyes remained locked with hers, deep pools of warmth that seemed to dive into her very soul, wordlessly expressing his love and devotion.

Dana felt the soft caress like a balm over the flush of her skin, the delicate contact sending a shiver through her despite the gentle nature of his touch. She leaned ever so slightly, her body instinctively seeking more of his warmth, her head tilting to accommodate the comforting hand that now cupped her face.

In the closeness of their shared space, she found security—a familiarity in the curve of his palm, the tender concern etched in the lines around his eyes. It was as if their bodies were old friends, reacquainting after a long journey apart, even though they had never truly been separated. Her shoulders relaxed, her guard down, melting into his presence as easily as sunlight dissolves into the horizon at dusk.

The air between them became something tangible, a cocoon woven from threads of silent understanding and raw emotions, holding them both in an embrace as powerful as any words could ever hope to convey.

Steven's lips sought hers, a gentle quest that Dana met with equal tenderness. Their breath mingled, a testament to the shared space between them that had grown intimate and sacred. As their mouths touched, soft and unhurried, there was a quiet acknowledgment of the passion they had ignited within each other. The simplicity of these kisses belied the depth of their connection; each one a whisper of every unspoken promise and longing that thrummed beneath their skin.

The taste of him was familiar—hints of the morning coffee still lingering on his tongue, mixed with something innately Steven that Dana found intoxicating. Her senses filled with the essence of him, a sensory anchor in the whirlwind of emotions that had swept through her since the night before. With each press of his lips to hers, she savored the sweetness and the strength that defined the man she loved.

Feeling her yield to his tender ministrations, Steven deepened their embrace, his arms wrapping around her in a silent vow of protection and care. His hold was firm yet gentle, as if he were cradling something precious and irreplaceable. Dana's heart swelled in response, a buoyant sensation that lifted her from within. In this moment, wrapped in Steven's arms, there was no judgment, no fear—only the pure solace that came from being held by the one who knew her soul.

Their bodies pressed together, the heat from their skin melding into a single warm glow that enveloped them both. Dana's fingers traced the muscles of Steven's back, feeling the steady beat of his heart against her chest. It was a rhythm that spoke of life, of love, of everything that they had endured and celebrated together. Here, entwined on their couch, they found refuge from the world outside—a sanctuary built on mutual respect, trust, and an unwavering bond that had only grown stronger with each new exploration of their hearts' deepest desires.

iii

The room was hushed, save for the soft rustle of fabric as Dana nestled closer to Steven. The ambient light from the window cast a warm glow over their interlocked forms on the couch. She tilted her head upward, her gaze meeting his with an intimacy that words often failed to capture.

"Last night," she began, her voice a whisper as if the very walls held secrets, "there was a moment when I felt..." She paused, searching for the right expression, "...unraveled, but in the most beautiful way. With Richard, it was like stepping off a cliff and knowing you'd be there to catch me."

Steven's thumb brushed against her hand, a silent acknowledgment of her trust. "It was intense," he agreed quietly, his eyes reflecting the flicker of emotions that danced between them. "Seeing you surrender, the way you let go... it was both exhilarating and terrifying."

Dana inhaled deeply, allowing the memories to flood through her senses. "And when he—" her voice broke off, a flush of reminiscence tinting her cheeks, "when he touched me, I felt like a chord was struck deep within, a note that only you've played before. It was unexpected, but it didn't scare me because I knew you were there."

"Every second," Steven whispered back, his eyes never leaving hers, "I saw your pleasure, your strength—it made everything else fade away.

I always want to give you the world, Dana, even if it means sharing parts of it with others."

"Thank you," she said, her voice laced with a depth of gratitude that swelled in her chest. "For trusting me."

Their whispers wove a tapestry of confession and affirmation, each thread pulling them tighter into the fabric of their shared life. Dana rested her head against Steven's shoulder, feeling the steady thump of his heart against her cheek, a rhythm that spoke of endless support and boundless exploration.

"Exploring these depths with you," Steven murmured, "is the greatest adventure. And wherever it leads, we'll face it together."

In the quiet sanctuary of their embrace, they continued to exchange soft-spoken dreams and desires, their conversation a private dance of words that celebrated the trust and love that had carried them to this point and would lead them into the future.

iv

The warmth of Steven's body seeped into Dana's skin, their legs tangled beneath the soft throw that draped over them, a gentle cocoon in the dim light of early evening. Her eyelids fluttered, heavy with the weight of shared confessions and a day spent chasing the edges of desire. His chest rose and fell in a slow, hypnotic rhythm, lulling her toward the brink of slumber.

A faint smile curved her lips as she nestled closer, her head finding the perfect nook under his chin. The room was silent, save for their synchronized breathing, and the occasional whisper of fabric as they shifted, seeking even more closeness. She felt the echo of his heartbeat against her palm, a steady drum that promised safety, a reminder of their unity.

In this tender tangle, every point where their bodies met sang a silent ode to intimacy. Their feet brushed together, toes idly caressing; knees fitted snug like the closing of a cherished book. Steven's arm, heavy and reassuring, draped across her waist, fingers splayed protectively, possessively, yet with an easiness that spoke of trust earned and given freely.

Their breathing deepened, each exhale a release of the day's tension, a sinking into mutual vulnerability that only true partners could share. The remnants of Richard's touch, once electric upon their skin, now simmered down to a warm, residual glow—a testament to the fires they had walked through and emerged from, not scorched, but radiant.

As sleep beckoned, Dana's consciousness teetered on the edge of dreams, the boundaries between reality and fantasy blurring. In those liminal spaces, images flickered behind closed lids: the arch of her back under Steven's gaze, the strength of his hands guiding her, the intensity of Richard's eyes unlocking something primal within her. The fantasies wove themselves into a tapestry of passion, each thread a memory, a possibility, a future exploration to be undertaken hand in hand with Steven.

The last coherent thought that drifted through Dana's mind before succumbing to the realm of dreams was a quiet acknowledgment of gratitude—for Steven, for their love that dared to expand, for the courage to embrace the depths of their desires together. With a final sigh, she let go, allowing the night to carry them both into reveries where their bond was celebrated, their connection stronger than ever, fortified by the trust that pulsed at the heart of their shared experience with Richard.

In slumber, their spirits danced, unrestrained and vivid, painting visions of a love unbound, a union that thrived on the thrill of discovery and the comfort found in each other's arms.

Part II

Exploration

CHAPTER 1

Three months had passed since their encounter with Richard, but the memory still lingered in Steven and Dana's minds like a faint whisper. As they fell back into their daily routine of work and keeping up with household tasks, a subtle tugging sensation began to grow beneath the surface. It was almost as if something was pulling at their souls, beckoning them towards a mysterious destination. Day by day, the calling became stronger, an alluring melody that they couldn't resist. Their minds were consumed with thoughts of this mysterious force drawing them closer.

Dana stood before the full-length mirror; her curvy silhouette wrapped in a sheer robe that clung to her figure like morning dew on a blushing peony. Her long, flowing blonde hair cascaded over her shoulders in waves, catching the light with every subtle movement and sending shimmering reflections dancing across the room. She traced the contours of her body with a delicate touch, each curve a testament to the womanly essence she both embodied and celebrated.

Beside her, Steven watched with a gaze that spoke volumes of their shared history—a blanket of comfort woven with threads of passion, trust, and the kind of love that transcends the mere physical. His short, dark hair was tousled just so, as if each strand had been coaxed into place by her own fingertips. His build, average transitioning into athletic from recent commitments to the gym, hinted at a dedication not only to his own health but to their collective vitality.

"Are you sure about this?" Steven's voice broke the silence, low and laced with a cocktail of anticipation and something else—something deeper, a silent acknowledgment of the adventures they'd embarked upon together.

"Richard opened a door for us," Dana replied, turning to face him, eyes alight with a flame that had been ignited one fateful evening and refused to be snuffed out. "It's not just curiosity, Steven—it's a journey. I feel it in my bones; we're meant to travel it."

Their previous encounter with Richard had been an unexpected revelation. It was supposed to be a one-time adventure, but as the night unfolded and the drinks flowed, boundaries blurred under the soft glow of dimmed lights and the intoxicating rhythm of suggestive dialogue. Richard, with his easy charm and smoldering eyes, had effortlessly enticed them into a daring dance of flirtation and subtle touches—an erotic prelude that left Dana and Steven breathless, craving more.

"Pushing limits," Steven murmured, echoing her thoughts as he stepped closer, bridging the gap between them until their bodies were mere inches apart. His hands settled on her waist, fingers splaying across the silk of her robe as if to claim and reassure all at once.

"Exploring desires," Dana countered, her voice a melodic whisper that seemed to resonate within the very walls of their sanctuary. She leaned into him, her lips parting in a silent invitation that needed no words.

"United," he finished for her, the single word a vow that sealed their mutual agreement to venture beyond the known. Their connection was their compass, guiding them through uncharted territories of pleasure and intimacy.

This exploration, born from an online encounter, was now theirs to shape—a path lined with the thrill of the unknown and the security of their unbreakable bond. Together, they would navigate the waters of desire, steering through the tides of power dynamics and control, always anchored by the deep love that pulsed steadfastly at the core of their union.

The flickering candlelight cast a dance of shadows across the bedroom, lending an air of anticipation to the conversation that hovered on the brink of decision. Dana perched on the edge of their bed, her fingertips tracing the intricate pattern on the duvet, a mimicry of the nerves fluttering in her belly. Steven watched her from the doorway, his silhouette a dark contrast against the soft glow of the hallway light.

"Imagine it," she said, her voice infused with a cocktail of trepidation and excitement, "a place where we can unleash these... these yearnings that Richard awoke within us."

Steven's footsteps were silent on the plush carpet as he approached, stopping at a respectful distance that belied the intimacy of their topic. "It's uncharted territory for us," he acknowledged, his eyes searching hers for any sign of hesitation, "but if we're together, I believe we can navigate anything."

"Even this?" Dana asked, her eyes wide pools reflecting the flame's quiver. There was a certain allure in the unknown—a siren call to the depths of their desires that neither could deny.

"Especially this," Steven confirmed, stepping closer until he was close enough for her to feel the warmth radiating from him. The air seemed charged with their shared curiosity, each breath they took lacing tighter the fabric of their resolve.

"Will you be okay with seeing me with someone else again?" Her question hung between them, weighted with the gravity of their commitment.

"Only if you are," he replied, reaching out to tuck a strand of her cascading blonde hair behind her ear. His touch was gentle, yet laden with the power he wielded in his promise to protect their bond above all else.

"Then let's do this," Dana decided, standing to meet his gaze levelly, the curves of her body outlined by the soft material of her robe. "Together."

"Always together," he echoed, his hand finding hers, their fingers interlocking in a physical manifestation of their unity.

ii

"WHAT HAVE YOU LEARNED about this club?" Steven asked.

Dana's eyes lit up as she recounted her conversation with the intriguing woman named Lila. "She promised me that all desires and interests are welcome and can be fulfilled at this place she told me about," Dana said excitedly. "It's like a combination nightclub and hotel, designed to cater to every desire."

Her words were punctuated by a wide grin as she described the different areas within the establishment. "There is a large dance floor, pulsating with music and bodies moving in rhythm, a sleek bar area for mingling and meeting new people, various themed rooms filled with mystery and possibility, quiet nooks for more intimate encounters, and private rooms that anyone could use to explore their wildest fantasies."

"And what's at the top of your list to discover first my dear?" Steven asked playfully.

"Mmm...I know you've been wanting to see me with a black man," Dana said with a seductive tone.

Steven replied confidently, "I have no doubt you will have no trouble attracting someone who catches your interest."

"Then let's see if we can find someone at the club," she purred.

Steven spoke with a serious tone, "We should decide on the rules we want to adhere to."

Dana replied, acknowledging his love for watching her, "But I'm still not comfortable with you being intimate with another woman. Am I being selfish?"

Steven's response was immediate and firm. "No way," he said, without a moment of hesitation. "I love seeing you content and satisfied. Our encounter with Richard only strengthened my desire to witness it again."

Dana replied with a nod, "That's settled then. Let's go find out what adventures the club has in store for us."

They stood there, husband and wife, bound by love and ignited by a mutual flame of exploration. Their decision was made—not out of haste, but from a deep-seated trust and open communication that had become the bedrock of their relationship. With their hands clasped and hearts synchronized, Dana and Steven stepped into the future—one of daring exploration at the swinger club, and beyond.

CHAPTER 2

The massive door creaked open, revealing a world of seduction and temptation hidden behind its imposing exterior. The ambience hit Dana and Steven like a wave, engulfing them in the intoxicating mix of musk and arousal. They stepped into the dimly lit space, bathed in hues of deep red and purple, the air thick with the promise of endless possibilities. The pulsating beat of music filled their ears and vibrated through their bodies, beckoning them further into this clandestine playground of desires.

Dana's heels clicked authoritatively against the polished floor. She felt the shift within her, from the woman who hesitated at the threshold to the embodiment of confidence that now navigated this sultry labyrinth.

The navy-blue dress hugged Dana's form like a shield, accentuating every curve and line of her body. The fabric shimmered in the dim light, catching every glint and casting her in a seductive glow.

As they ventured deeper into the dimly lit club, she could feel eyes on her, sizing her up and undressing her with their gaze. The crowd was a mix of leather-clad dominatrixes, suited businessmen, and seductive dancers in fishnet stockings. Each person exuded an air of confidence and desire, and she basked in their attention as if it were a cloak of empowerment. She knew that this was the place to let go of all inhibitions and indulge in the carnal pleasures promised by the night ahead

Steven's hand, a subtle heat upon the velvet of Dana's bare back, was both an anchor and a compass. It whispered along her spine with the faintest pressure, steering them through the throng of bodies that ebbed and flowed like an exotic sea around them. The gesture, small as it may have been, spoke volumes of his desire in its possessiveness, the way his fingers splayed over the curve of her lower back as if to claim her amidst the cacophony of silent yearnings that filled the room.

The club unfurled before them, a painted canvas of human desires brushed in broad strokes of skin and fabric. Eyes trailing the scene, Dana's attention was once again drawn to the sea of seductive clothing that adorned the attendees - a chaotic mix of lace, leather, and even less. Women glimmered with delicately draped chains and transparent fabrics, their bodies serving as alluring canvases for eager gazes.

Each person they passed seemed to be an emissary from a world where inhibition was a forgotten currency. A woman with hair the color of midnight sauntered by, her corset cinched tightly, accentuating an hourglass figure that defied time itself. Nearby, a man whose bare chest was a mural of ink leaned languidly against a pillar, his gaze locked on Dana with an intensity that promised untold stories.

"Incredible," Steven murmured, his breath a soft exhalation against her ear, though whether he spoke of her or the crowd, Dana couldn't be certain.

"Intoxicating," she replied, the word rolling off her tongue like a drop of honey, slow and deliberate. Her voice carried a tremor of excitement that vibrated between them, a shared secret that pulsed in time with the music.

Dana felt the pull of Steven's presence, a gravitational force that held her steady even as the world around them swirled with the promise of pleasure and discovery. His touch was a constant reminder that while they were adventurers on the precipice of an erotic abyss, they were tethered to each other, bound by the silent vows they had woven into the fabric of their union.

Their journey through the club continued, each step a descent into deeper realms of sensation and spectacle, where every glance held an invitation and every smile was a prelude to ecstasy. And all the while, Steven's hand remained on Dana's back, a silent testament to his simmering desire, guiding her confidently towards the unknown pleasures that awaited them.

The pulse of the music seemed to synchronize with the rhythm of conversation, a melodic undertone to the symphony of soft chuckles and sultry whispers that enveloped Dana and Steven as they threaded through the crowd. Every word exchanged was ripe with innuendo, each laugh a note of complicity in the night's unfolding decadence.

"Care for a taste?" A voice, thick with suggestion, teased from somewhere to their left, followed by a playful giggle that danced on the edge of scandalous.

"Only if you can handle the flavor," another voice riposted, bold and brazen.

Dana's ears tingled with these verbal caresses, each one painting strokes of audacity and allure upon the canvas of her imagination. The club's atmosphere was drenched in the perfume of possibility, where boundaries were mere suggestions waiting to be crossed, and every exchange was an overture to deeper indulgence.

Steven led her past a pair of bodies wrapped in conversation, so close they seemed to breathe as one. The man leaned in, his words a velvet murmur only inches from his companion's ear, eliciting a shiver that ran visibly down her spine, a silent ode to the power of whispered promises.

"Discoveries around every corner," Steven noted, his tone laced with the excitement of exploration as his eyes roved over the landscape of flesh and fantasy before them.

"Indeed," Dana replied, her voice threaded with the thrill of witnessing such uninhibited displays. She could sense the charge in the air, a current that coursed through the club, igniting sparks of desire at the brush of skin against skin or the meeting of strangers' gazes.

They passed by an enclave where shadows caressed silhouettes engaged in a dance of seduction. The light played upon entwined figures, casting an ethereal glow upon the curves and contours of those who had surrendered to the evening's temptations, their movements a sensual choreography of mutual yearning.

"Everywhere, energy," Dana breathed out, almost to herself, entranced by the display of passion and playfulness that stretched out around them. In this electric ambience, every glance held weight, every touch carried charge, and the very air vibrated with the palpable intensity of connections being forged and fantasies being chased.

With Steven's guiding hand ever-present, they navigated this labyrinth of longing, each step taking them deeper into a realm where the only currency was pleasure, and the only rule was to give in to the magnetic pull of raw, unfettered desire.

ii

DANA'S PULSE THRUMMED in her ears, a syncopated rhythm to the club's throbbing bass. She felt the heat of curious eyes skimming over her, each gaze igniting a flicker of excitement that danced nervously along her spine. The very air seemed to shimmer with intrigue, each glance from passing strangers a silent conversation filled with hidden meanings and unspoken promises.

"Are you alright?" Steven's voice was low, a gentle undercurrent beneath the cascade of sound around them. His concern was a grounding force in the whirlwind of sensory overload.

"More than alright," she confessed, her words tinged with a breathless quality. She was buoyant amidst the sea of temptation, carried on waves of curiosity that lapped at the shores of her arousal. Every look shared with another added fuel to the fire of her imagination, painting vivid scenarios that blushed her cheeks with their boldness.

Steven's touch, a soft pressure at the base of her back, was both a compass and an anchor — subtle yet commanding. It steered her through the throng of bodies with the ease of an unspoken covenant between them. His fingertips grazed the exposed skin where her dress dipped into a low V, sending ripples of warmth cascading down her body, a silent reminder of his presence and protection amidst the fervor.

"Stay close," he murmured, though it was less a command and more a confession of his need for her proximity, his longing for her as palpable as the charged atmosphere that enveloped them.

"Of course," Dana breathed in return, leaning subtly into his caress. Each brush of his hand against her was a language unto itself, speaking volumes of their bond, reinforcing their unity even as they stood on the precipice of untold adventures. His fingers traced patterns of assurance and possession along her spine, mapping out territories known only to them even as they ventured further into the unknown.

The dance of glances continued, a visual waltz that Dana found herself partaking in with a mixture of trepidation and thrill. She was a canvas of desire, her nerves the fine bristles of a brush painting strokes of yearning with every heartbeat. Steven was the artist, his touches guiding the masterpiece they created together, one of trust, exploration, and the deepening hue of shared fantasies waiting to be fulfilled.

Dana's dress clung to her like a provocative second skin, the fabric delineating each voluptuous curve with an intention that left little to the imagination. The sleek design seemed to capture and amplify the club's ambient lighting, casting a subtle glow upon her figure as she moved through the throngs of onlookers. With every step, the hem whispered against her thighs, the sensation a constant whisper of silk that teased her senses, reminding her of the liberties she was allowing herself this night.

The attention Dana drew was palpable, a tangible caress that skated along her bare shoulders and dipped daringly into the valley of her back. Both men and women watched her passage, their gazes lingering in silent appreciation, igniting a simmering excitement within her. It was as if her presence alone issued a siren's call, stirring the desires of those she passed by, beckoning them to imagine the secrets hidden beneath the elegant facade of her attire.

Steven felt the shift in the air, the way eyes tracked his wife's every sway and sashay. His hand, previously content to linger at the small of Dana's back, now tightened ever so slightly. It was a move almost imperceptible to anyone but her, a silent statement of claim that resonated deep within her core. Steven's fingers pressed with gentle authority, drawing her body closer to his until they were seamlessly aligned, his warmth a solid reassurance against the coolness of strangers' appraisals.

"Exquisite," he murmured into her ear, his breath a hot contrast to the chill that danced upon her skin from the club's air. The word rolled off his tongue, heavy with implication and promise, a singular accolade that spoke of the beauty she radiated and the desire it summoned within him.

"Am I?" Dana's voice held a note of playful defiance, mingled with a vulnerability that only he could recognize. Her question was both an affirmation and a dare, challenging him to affirm her power over him even as they stood enveloped by the carnivorous gaze of others.

"Beyond words," he assured her, his lips brushing the shell of her ear in a kiss so fleeting it might have been a figment of her heated imagination. But it wasn't. It was real, as real as the possessive grip that now slid down to encircle her waist, Steven's thumb tracing the outline of her ribs through the thin material of her dress. His hold was a silent dialogue, speaking volumes of possession and protection, a leash of love and lust that bound them amidst the sea of possibility.

Each touch from Steven was a lifeline, an anchor that kept her grounded even as her mind wandered to the tantalizing 'what ifs' that fluttered around them like moths to flame. The duality of her desires—the thrill of being admired and the comfort found in his claim—wove a complex tapestry of arousal that cloaked her in its intricate designs.

As Dana leaned into the safety of Steven's embrace, she allowed herself to revel in the dual sensations of exposure and enclosure, her body a beacon in the night that drew hungry eyes while her heart beat securely in the cage of his arms.

Dana inhaled deeply; the air thick with an intoxicating cocktail of scents that clung to her senses like a second skin. Perfume and cologne warred with the natural musk of bodies in motion, each fragrance a heady note in an olfactory symphony that spoke of forbidden pleasures and unspoken invitations. The aroma of sweat — the sheen of exertion and excitement — blended seamlessly with the softer, more intimate scent of arousal that seemed to emanate from every shadowed nook of the club. It was an invisible haze, a pheromonal fog that wrapped around Dana and Steven, urging them closer to the precipice of their own desires.

"Can you feel it?" Steven's voice was a low rumble against her ear, his breath a warm contrast to the coolness of her flushed skin. His question was rhetorical, needling at the core of her heightened awareness.

"Everywhere," she murmured back, her lips barely moving as if afraid to release the potent energy building within her.

They continued their journey through the pulsating heart of the club, Steven's hand never leaving the small of Dana's back, fingers splayed as though claiming every inch of her they touched. The thrumming beat of the music now seemed distant, secondary to the rhythm of their synchronized heartbeats. With each step, Dana felt as if they were drawing away from the cacophony, retreating into a world that belonged solely to them.

Eventually, they found themselves at the edge of a quiet corner, the dim lighting casting a seductive glow on the plush velvet of an inviting chaise. The relative seclusion was a stark contrast to the vibrancy they had left behind, yet the hum of the club still reverberated through the walls, a silent reminder of the world that awaited them just beyond their sanctuary.

"Here...," Steven whispered, his hand leaving her back only to extend towards the chaise, inviting her to sit.

Dana settled onto the soft fabric, her legs crossing demurely as she looked up at Steven standing before her. In this quiet corner, the power dynamics shifted subtly. No longer surrounded by prying eyes, the decision of what came next lay firmly in their hands. The anticipation between them crackled, a living entity that danced in their locked gazes.

"Are you ready for this?" Steven asked, the simple query laden with the weight of all they had witnessed and all that could be.

"More than anything," Dana replied, her voice steady despite the flutter in her chest. "With you."

Steven sat beside her, close enough for their thighs to touch, a silent affirmation of their shared eagerness to explore the depths of their connection. Here in the dim light, the rest of the world fell away, leaving only the two of them perched on the edge of discovery.

"Then let's begin," he said, his hand finding hers, their fingers intertwining like vines seeking purchase in new, fertile ground.

Dana and Steven sat together in their chosen alcove; their bodies poised like sculptures awaiting the artist's first transformative stroke. The club around them faded into a backdrop, a stage set for the play they were about to write with their own hands, hearts, and whispered promises of pleasure yet to come.

CHAPTER 3

The thrumming heartbeat of the club pulsed through the dimly lit room, a symphony of whispered desires and the soft clink of glasses. Dana's grip on Steven's hand tightened, her breath hitching as she scanned the sea of bodies, each moving with an intoxicating blend of grace and carnal promise. Amidst this dance of anticipation, Lila Thompson emerged like a siren from the depths, her confident stride parting the crowd as she approached the couple.

Lila's lithe figure was adorned in a sleek, form-fitting black dress, creating a striking silhouette against the backdrop of the room. Her long, cascading waves of hair, black as the night sky, swayed with each step she took. The icy blue depths of her eyes seemed to hold a thousand untold secrets, drawing in anyone who dared to meet her gaze. As she stood before Dana and Steven, her body exuded a magnetic confidence, beckoning them closer with promises of forbidden pleasures waiting to be discovered.

"Hello there," Lila's voice was a velvet purr that seemed to vibrate in tune with the club's rhythm. "I'm Lila. You must be Dana and Steven. I can see the excitement in your eyes—and perhaps a touch of trepidation?"

Dana's lips parted, but no words came forth, her throat tight with a cocktail of nerves and thrill. It was Steven, his curiosity gilded with an adventurous glint, who nodded. "That obvious, huh?"

"Only to an experienced eye," Lila responded, her gaze never wavering, her smile warm yet edged with something more enigmatic. She leaned in slightly, her presence enveloping them in a cocoon of assurance and allure. "This place... it can be overwhelming at first. But fear not, I'm here to guide you through it, to share what I've learned."

"Really?" Dana found her voice, a whisper that betrayed her vulnerability. "You'd do that for us?"

"Of course." Lila's response was immediate, her hand gesturing towards the labyrinthine space around them. "Think of me as your sherpa through these peaks of pleasure and valleys of desire. Everyone here had a first time, filled with questions and hunger for exploration. I remember mine well."

Steven's posture relaxed a fraction, the initial tension subsiding under Lila's calming influence. "We'd appreciate any help you can offer," he said, a newfound steadiness to his tone.

"Consider me at your service then." Lila's assurance was as tangible as the electric air that surrounded them, her willingness to aid the novice pair in navigating the complexities of their surroundings shining through with genuine enthusiasm.

"Thank you," Dana murmured, the sincerity in her gaze reflecting both her gratitude and the burgeoning confidence that Lila's presence inspired. "We're grateful for your kindness."

"Think nothing of it," Lila replied, her lips curving in a way that suggested shared secrets and the promise of untold stories. "After all, we're all here in search of something... aren't we?"

Lila leaned in, her gaze locking onto Dana's with an intensity that seemed to draw out the very secrets of her soul. "Tell me, "She began, her voice a low purr that vibrated through the charged atmosphere, "what is it that you're yearning for tonight? And remember, honesty is the key that unlocks the most exquisite experiences."

Dana hesitated, her lips parting slightly as if the words were on the brink of spilling forth. She glanced at Steven, seeking reassurance before confessing, "I... we're curious. About everything, really. But it's important to us that we respect each other's limits."

"Of course," Lila nodded, her attention shifting to Steven, inviting him into the fold of their intimate conversation. "And what about you, Steven? What boundaries do we need to be mindful of as we embark on this journey?"

Steven's throat moved as he swallowed, his unwavering gaze fixed on Lila. "We've discussed it," he spoke with calmness, but his racing pulse revealed his true emotions. "I have a strong desire to witness Dana experiencing pleasure. She's not comfortable with the idea of me being intimate with another woman, but she is free to explore any desires she may have."

"Very reasonable and common," Lila commented, her tone warm and approving. "Establishing clear boundaries is crucial here. It ensures that the thrill of desire doesn't overshadow mutual respect."

She gestured around them, her movements fluid and deliberate. "This club is a sanctuary of sorts. A place where fantasies take flight, where pleasure is both given and received freely." Lila's eyes sparkled with the promise of hidden knowledge as she continued. "There are rooms that cater to every whim – from the soft caress of silk in the Sensory Suite to the exhilarating dominance of the Red Chamber. Each space has its own etiquette, its own unspoken language of consent and control."

Dana absorbed the words, the imagery painting vivid strokes across the canvas of her imagination. "It sounds... overwhelming," she admitted, the trepidation and excitement mingling in her voice.

"Perhaps at first," Lila agreed, her smile reassuring. "But you'll find that the pulse of this place beats in rhythm with your own desires. Should you choose the Viewing Gallery, know that eyes may follow your dance of passion, yet only from a distance, unless you invite them closer. In the Mirror Maze, reflections tell a thousand tales, each glance a silent conversation between spectators and participants."

"Is there a secret to navigating all this?" Steven asked, his curiosity piqued by Lila's depiction of the club's possibilities.

"Listen to your instincts," she advised, leaning back to study them both, her expression serene yet intense. "Communicate with one another. And never hesitate to say 'no' or 'yes', as your hearts and bodies dictate. The staff here are vigilant guardians of safety and consent; they'll intervene should any situation require it."

"Thank you, Lila," Dana said softly, the weight of uncertainty lifting as understanding dawned. "Your words... they make it seem less daunting."

"Your pleasure is my pleasure," Lila responded, her voice laced with sincerity and a hint of something deeper, more enigmatic. "Remember, I'm here to guide you, to help you navigate these waters of liberation and desire. Simply seek me out. Now, go on, explore and please do let me know if you need anything at all," Lila urged, her smile both a challenge and a blessing. "Let the night unveil its wonders to you. I'll be here, watching the stars align in your favor."

With that, Lila stepped back, allowing them space to breathe, to contemplate the path that lay ahead. As she watched Dana and Steven exchange a look of shared courage, she knew they were ready to begin their own odyssey into the depths of their unexplored passions.

With hearts buoyed by anticipation, Dana and Steven rose from their seats. Their steps were surer now, each stride a testament to the newfound confidence that Lila had nurtured within them. They ventured deeper into the swirling milieu of the club, the air rich with the scent of desire and the warmth of bodies moving in unison.

The promise of what lay ahead was a siren song, luring them toward the exploration of not just flesh, but the very essence of their connection. And with Lila's guidance still echoing in their minds, Dana and Steven stepped forward, ready to dance along the edge of their boundaries, to taste the sweet nectar of liberation that only true surrender could bring.

ii

DANA'S HAND FOUND STEVEN'S in the dimly lit corridor, her fingers threading through his with a squeeze that spoke of shared courage. The pulsating beat from the club's main room grew distant as they moved away from the sanctuary Lila had provided, toward the unknown pleasures that beckoned them deeper into the labyrinth.

"Are you ready?" she whispered, her voice a mix of trepidation and yearning.

Steven's response was a gentle tug forward, leading her with an assurance that belied the rapid thud of his own heart. "As long as I'm with you," he murmured back, his dark eyes holding hers with an intensity that made her pulse race.

The hallway opened up into a spacious area, where the glow of crimson lights cast a seductive hue over entwined bodies. The air hummed with the energy of raw desire, a tangible force that settled on Dana's skin like velvet, urging her to shed the last of her inhibitions.

They paused, taking in the sight before them—a mosaic of sensuality that painted every shade of passion and longing. Dana felt the stirrings within her awaken fully, a bloom of heat that unfurled at the core of her being.

"Whatever happens tonight," Steven said, his voice low and steady, "we are in this together. Our journey, our rules."

Dana nodded, her blonde hair cascading over her shoulders as she leaned into him for a kiss that sealed their silent pact. It was a kiss not of possession but of promise—the sort that fortified bonds and fanned the flames of mutual exploration.

As they broke apart, they took a collective breath, stepping forward into the throng. With each step, the fabric of reality seemed to thin, the veil between their everyday lives and this night of hedonistic pursuit growing ever more transparent.

Together, they roamed, eyes wide with wonder, each new room a revelation of sights and sounds that tested the limits of their fantasies. Hands brushed against skin, whispers filled their ears—offers and invitations hanging ripe in the air.

And though the temptation swirled around them, it was the silent conversation between Dana and Steven that held the true power. In their glances and touches, they communicated their readiness, their consent, their trust. It was a dance of nods and subtle smiles, a choreography that only they understood.

Through it all, the presence of Lila lingered like a guardian muse, her words a talisman that reminded them of the strength they held together. They were not merely adrift in this sea of carnality; they were navigators, charting their own course through the waters of want and will.

"Let's discover," Dana finally said, her voice a breathless caress against Steven's ear. "Let's discover everything." Her green eyes sparkled with the reflections of the club's lights, but it was the inner light of her own awakening that truly illuminated her face.

"I'll follow your lead," Steven repeated, holding her hand tightly as they moved forward.

And with that affirmation, they delved deeper into the heart of the club, two souls embarked upon a voyage that would unfurl the sails of their hidden depths, setting them adrift on the vast ocean of erotic discovery.

CHAPTER 4

Amidst the writhing bodies and carnal desires, Dana's gaze was fixated on one particular patron. Her heart hammered against her ribcage, a wild symphony of desire and longing at the sight of Marcus across the dimly lit room. He stood tall and proud, a dominant figure amidst the haze of lust and shadows, drawing her in with an irresistible magnetism. Steven's hand pressed firmly against her back, a silent gesture that fueled her determination.

The air between them seemed to crackle, charged with the electricity of unspoken promises as their eyes locked—a silent communion that spoke volumes. Each step she took toward Marcus felt like shedding a layer of her former self, emboldened by the raw hunger mirrored in his gaze.

"Go on," Steven murmured, almost lost in the pulsing music around them. His words were a gentle nudge, propelling her into the unknown.

As Dana's eyes hungrily traced Marcus' lean, dark, muscular frame, she felt a surge of desire wash over her. His broad shoulders tapered into a trim waist, accentuating the powerful muscles rippling beneath his taut skin. With each step he took towards her, his body exuded a primal aura that left her breathless. A sly grin spread across his chiseled jawline, teasing at the primal instincts within Dana and making her pulse race with anticipation.

"Seems like fate has a plan for us tonight," Marcus said, his voice a low rumble that resonated within her.

"Or maybe it's just good timing," Dana replied, her voice tinged with a boldness that surprised even herself. The playful twinkle in her eye was a silent challenge, an invitation to dance on the edge of propriety.

Their conversation became a delicate waltz of words, each phrase laced with innuendo that hung heavy in the air between them, tantalizing and ripe with possibility. When his hand brushed against hers, a spark ignited, the touch whisper-light yet searing in its intensity.

"Careful now," Marcus teased, his fingers grazing the inside of her wrist, "I might think you're leading me into temptation."

"Wouldn't dream of it," she quipped, though her breath hitched at the contact, betraying her cool exterior.

His laughter was a deep, melodic sound that seemed to vibrate through the thrumming bass of the club. "Somehow, I doubt that," he countered, his eyes gleaming with mischief.

"Maybe I'm just exploring my options," Dana flirted back, leaning in so the curve of her body hinted at the contours hidden beneath her dress, offering a subtle promise of the delights it concealed.

"Exploration is key," Marcus agreed, his fingertips tracing an invisible line up her arm, sending shivers cascading down her spine. "Finding out what treasures might be buried... just beneath the surface."

In this moment, as they stood wrapped in their cocoon of charged repartee, Dana found herself carried away by the current of desire, ready to relinquish control to the magnetic pull of Marcus's confidence.

Marcus leaned in, his breath a warm whisper against the shell of Dana's ear. "You look like a woman who knows exactly what she wants but is just a little afraid to seize it," he murmured, his voice a velvet caress that seemed to stroke her very soul.

Dana shivered as the timbre of his words reverberated through her, an intimate vibration that unsettled yet thrilled her. The heat of his body was a magnetic field pulling her closer into his orbit, and she fought to keep her breathing steady, to not let on how deeply his proximity affected her.

"Maybe I'm waiting for the right guide," she managed to reply, her voice threaded with a desire that felt both foreign and exhilarating. The words tumbled from her lips, daring and bold, encouraged by the illicit excitement of their situation.

"Then let me chart the course," he said, his hand resting lightly at the small of her back, a promise of control and protection all at once. His touch was both a question and an answer, igniting fires along nerve endings she hadn't known were so parched for the flames.

Dana turned her face slightly, her cheek brushing against the rough stubble of his jaw, feeling the solid reality of him. There was a power in his stance, a certainty in his grip, that drew her in. She tilted her head back to meet his gaze, her eyes darkening with unspoken promises and a hint of challenge. Her lips parted just so, an invitation hanging between them without a single word.

"Is this part of the exploration?" Her tone was playful yet laced with an edge, one that flirted with daring him to push further, to test the boundaries they had only begun to sketch out in this dance of flirtation.

"Every discovery begins with a single step," Marcus replied, his fingers pressing ever so slightly into her back, guiding her closer into the charged space that sizzled around them. His eyes locked onto hers, a silent command that beckoned her deeper into the labyrinth of sensation they were weaving together.

The club around them faded into a blur, the pounding music a distant thunder compared to the racing of her heart. In this moment, with Marcus's whispers painting a portrait of latent desire, Dana found herself on the precipice of surrender, captivated by the allure of the unknown that he represented. The thrill of the chase, the hunger in his eyes—it all fused into a potent lure that Dana found herself powerless to resist.

ii

"COME WITH ME." MARCUS whispered.

Dana flicked a glance back at Steven, her eyes filled with questions. He gave her a subtle nod and she refocused her attention on Marcus, eager to unravel the mystery that lay ahead.

Marcus's hand, warm and commanding, enclosed Dana's with an assurance that spoke of the journey they were about to embark on. He led her through the labyrinthine club, his pace deliberate, each step a silent promise of the indulgence that awaited. The throng of bodies parted for him, as if even the air recognized his dominion over this realm of carnal delights.

Through a partially ajar door, a sliver of forbidden tableau revealed itself—a couple entwined in the throes of unbridled passion. Their bodies were a tangled web of limbs and curves, moving in perfect synchrony as their moans filled the room like a symphony of primal desire. Dana's eyes were drawn to the scene, mesmerized by the raw intensity and longing she saw in their faces. She could feel Marcus's warm breath against her neck as he leaned in closer, his voice a smooth velvet caress that sent shivers down her spine.

Marcus extended an invitation, his voice laced with temptation. "Watch them with me," he whispered, "and imagine it is you in that room, the ecstasy of giving in to your desires without restraint. Letting the world witness the raw power of your pleasure."

Dana's gaze lingered, transfixed by the raw display of sensuality. The woman's body was a symphony of curves and dips, each movement a masterful stroke of the brush, creating a canvas of pleasure that begged to be touched and explored. Dana watched as she writhed under her partner's skilled hands. Her arching back and gasping breaths were a testament to the art of touch, creating peaks of pleasure on the canvas of flesh before them. As she stood there, unable to tear her eyes away,

Dana felt a stirring inside her - was it curiosity or something deeper? Whatever it was, it kept her rooted to the spot, her own breath hitching in anticipation.

"Could you lose yourself like that?" Marcus teased, his tone dancing on the edge of provocation. "Could you be that woman, savoring every sensation under my guidance?"

She swallowed hard, her pulse echoing the couple's crescendo as she watched them crest the wave of climax, their bodies shuddering in seismic bliss. It was a mirror to her own burgeoning need, a need that Marcus was all too adept at stoking.

With the couple's cries still hanging in the air, Marcus guided her away, his touch a lodestone pulling her towards a tranquility that contrasted sharply with the fervor they left behind. They found sanctuary on a plush leather couch secluded from prying eyes, the material cool against Dana's skin, a balm to the fire that raged within her.

"Comfortable?" His question was laced with an undercurrent of control, and although he sat beside her, the space between them buzzed with the energy of unspoken intentions.

"Yes," she replied, her voice a soft tremor betraying the tumult inside her. In the dim light, his eyes were deep pools of intent, drawing her into depths where only the brave—or the reckless—dared to swim.

Here, in this quiet corner, the dance of dominance and surrender continued, the crescendo of their earlier encounter giving way to a new rhythm—one of anticipation, of the slow build that promised to eclipse anything Dana had ever known.

iii

MARCUS'S FINGERS TRAILED the bare skin of Dana's arm, a mere whisper of touch that sent her senses into overdrive. The leather of the couch creaked softly as he shifted closer, their voices a symphony of low murmurs lost in the ambient hum of the club's distant revelry.

"Tell me," Marcus's voice was smooth, a dark chocolate timbre that seemed to resonate with her very soul, "what is it you're seeking here tonight?"

The question, though simple, seemed boundless, echoing the labyrinthine paths of her deepest desires. She hesitated, not from uncertainty but from the sheer magnitude of her want. His gaze held her captive, and she found herself leaning into his gravitational pull, allowing her body to answer for her.

"Exploration," she breathed out, her words less a declaration and more an invocation spoken at the altar of newfound possibilities.

Marcus's smile was the curve of a new horizon, and his hand, now on her knee, began a leisurely ascent, mapping out the contours of her thigh with the softness of a cartographer charting undiscovered lands. Each touch was a promise, an assurance of pleasures yet to be claimed.

"Exploration," he repeated, his tone dipping into the octave of raw desire, "is a journey best embarked upon together."

Their conversation ebbed away as physical language took precedence. His hand, emboldened, traced the hemline of her dress, teasing the fabric upwards, exposing inch by tantalizing inch of skin warmed by the flush of arousal.

Dana's breath hitched, her chest rising and falling with tides of need that threatened to submerge her. In his presence, she felt alive, every nerve ending alight with a yearning that begged to be sated.

It was then Marcus leaned in, the heat of his breath cascading over the shell of her ear before his lips brushed against hers—a touch feather-light yet laden with intent. The kiss deepened, a convergence of passion that melded them together, two figures etching a moment of pure connection amidst the backdrop of a world forgotten.

Their bodies pressed close, the contours of Marcus's muscular frame complimenting the curves of her own, as if they were sculpted to fit one another. His hand cradled her face, thumb caressing her cheekbone, while his other arm encircled her waist, drawing her ever nearer.

In the cocoon of their embrace, amid the heady scent of longing that surrounded them, Dana surrendered to the sensations overwhelming her. Power dynamics played out in the tender duel of their tongues, in the give and take of breaths mingled, and in the silent dance of dominance and submission that thrummed beneath their skin.

This was not just a kiss. It was an awakening, a seismic shift in the tectonics of her being that redefined the boundaries of her pleasure, of her willingness to explore the uncharted territories that Marcus promised with every deliberate, intoxicating movement of his lips against hers.

Marcus's hand, once content with gentle exploration, grew bolder in its journey across the landscape of Dana's body. His fingertips traced the rise and fall of her curves, a cartographer charting the terrains of desire that quivered beneath her skin. Each assertive stroke of his touch was like a spark to kindling, flames licking through her veins, setting alight a fire that had been dormant for far too long.

"Does this feel good?" Marcus's voice was a low rumble, resonating with the power that seemed to radiate from him, enveloping her in a cocoon of yearning.

"More than good," Dana breathed out, the words catching in her throat as his fingers found the small of her back, pressing firmly, urging her closer into his embrace.

The heat of Marcus's body was a beacon, drawing her in, even as the specter of guilt clawed at the edges of her mind. She was married, devoted to Steven, yet here she was, melting into the arms of another man, allowing herself to be remolded by the hands of someone who wasn't her husband. The guilt should have been a deterrent, a stronghold against the onslaught of pleasure, but Marcus's commanding presence dismantled her defenses brick by brick.

"Let go," he whispered against the sensitive skin just below her earlobe, sending shivers cascading down her spine. "Forget everything else. Just feel."

Dana's internal battle waged on, a tempest of desire clashing against the stalwart cliffs of fidelity. But the sensation of Marcus's body aligned with hers, the strength in his touch, the intoxicating assurance in his every move—it all beckoned her toward a precipice she'd never dared approach before. And as she teetered on the brink, it was the overwhelming pleasure, the electric connection that surged between them, that tipped the scales.

With a surrender that felt like falling and flying all at once, Dana allowed the tidal wave of desire to wash over her, carrying away the remnants of her resistance. In Marcus's arms, she found an unexpected harbor, a place where the storms of guilt subsided into ripples upon the surface of a newfound ocean—a depth of passion and control that promised to drown her in its depths and buoy her to heights untold.

Marcus leaned in, the warmth of his breath a stark contrast to the pulse-thumping rhythm of the music that filled the club's air. His lips hovered just above the shell of her ear, and his voice, a velvet rumble, spilled forth with intimate promises.

"Imagine it," he murmured, his words laced with seduction. "You, uninhibited and radiant, basking in the glow of pure ecstasy."

She felt him shift, his presence an enveloping cocoon that teased the edges of her awareness. The subtle brush of his fingertips trailed down her arm, weightless yet laden with unspoken intentions.

"Can you feel it?" He continued, painting a picture so vivid she could almost touch it. "The heat of my hands as I explore the secrets of your skin; the pleasure that spirals from a simple caress."

Dana's pulse quickened, each beat echoing Marcus's words, and with every syllable, the room seemed to grow dimmer, the world outside their bubble fading into obscurity. She clung to his words; a lifeline thrown amidst the stormy sea of her longing.

"Picture yourself surrendering to sensation, to the sweet tension building within," he whispered, his fingers now tracing the outline of her collarbone, a path charted for discovery.

Her breath hitched, caught between reality and the tantalizing fantasy Marcus wove around her. The boundaries she had clung to started to blur; the lines smudged by his expert articulation of desire.

"Let me take you there. To a place where only our senses dictate the truth, where your pleasure is the sole commandment I abide by." His hand rested at the small of her back, a grounding force yet a silent ruler of her yielding form.

With his words, he painted landscapes of passion across the canvas of her mind, each stroke a deliberate play of power and persuasion. In this dance of dialogue, Marcus was both the artist and the maestro, coaxing her deeper into the realm of what could be.

"Feel the strength of my grip," he coaxed, "the control that guides you to peaks that linger on the horizon of your imagination, waiting to be conquered."

And in that moment, Dana felt herself teetering on the edge of that peak, gazing into the abyss of unfathomable depths. With Marcus, the fear of falling was usurped by the exhilarating promise of what lay beyond the fall—freedom in surrender, power in yielding.

"Trust in me, in the journey I want to share with you," he said, his voice a silken thread weaving through her defenses, pulling them apart one filament at a time.

In the sanctuary of Marcus's words, Dana found a liberation that beckoned her forward, urging her to cast off the shackles of hesitation. Here, in the charged space between them, she glimpsed the allure of a world where control was both taken and given, where the language of bodies spoke louder than words, and where desire was the currency of connection.

"Give in to it," he breathed out, his tone a mix of command and entreaty. "Let me show you how exquisite letting go can truly be."

And as the last vestiges of her resistance melted away under the heat of his whispered enticements, Dana realized that sometimes, the most powerful act of defiance was to submit to the desires of one's own heart.

CHAPTER 5

Marcus broke the spell of their kiss. The flickering candlelight cast a warm glow on the private alcove, creating an intimate sphere where Marcus and Dana sat facing each other. The air was thick with unspoken promises, each breath laced with the heady scent of anticipation. Marcus leaned in, the space between them shrinking as his presence enveloped her. His voice was a low rumble, stirring the silence like a caress against bare skin.

"Tell me, "He said, his breath hot upon her cheek, "what are the fantasies that dance through your mind when the world falls away?"

Dana's heart galloped in her chest; her senses heightened by the nearness of him. She fought to maintain composure, even as her body betrayed her, leaning subtly into his magnetic field. She felt the weight of his gaze, dark eyes holding her own, compelling her truth to surface.

"I... I've always been curious about power," she confessed, her voice a trembling whisper. Her fingers twisted in her lap, betraying the turmoil within. "The push and pull of it—the idea of surrendering to someone strong, someone like you."

Marcus's lips curled into a knowing smile, one that spoke of secrets shared and understood. He didn't break eye contact, seeking her soul with his stare as much as her spoken desires.

"Control can be a delicious burden," he mused softly. "And submission? A liberation unlike any other. To give oneself over to another's command, to trust so deeply that you allow your very pleasure to be governed... It's a powerful exchange, my dear."

Her breath hitched at his words, the suggestion of surrender igniting a flame deep within her. With every syllable, he wove the web tighter around her, the threads of dominance and submission intertwining in the air that mingled between them.

"Would you trust me to take you there?" Marcus asked, his voice a velvet stroke against the tender shell of her ear.

Dana nodded, captivated by the promise in his eyes, her body yearning for the tether of his control. In this cloistered space, amid the shadows and whispers, she felt the confines of her former self begin to unravel, making room for the awakening desires he summoned forth with every word.

Marcus leaned back slightly, the intensity of his gaze never waning. "Your honesty calls to me," he said, his voice a low rumble that vibrated with restrained power. "I too crave the dance of dominance and submission—the raw beauty of guiding and being guided."

Dana's heart raced as she listened, her skin prickling with anticipation. She felt exposed yet safe, as if Marcus had peeled away her layers without stripping her bare.

"Imagine my hands," Marcus continued, "strong and sure, claiming you. They would chart a course over your body, leaving no inch untouched, no whisper of desire unexplored." His hand lifted, drifting through the air as though caressing an invisible canvas.

Dana's breath caught in her throat, her imagination painting vivid strokes upon her skin where his words suggested. The very idea of his touch was like a flame to tinder within her.

"Your pleasure," he said, leaning forward again, his voice a silken thread weaving through her senses, "would be my command. Every moan, every shiver under my touch, would be a signpost, guiding me to your ultimate surrender."

His hand again found her knee, a simple touch that held the promise of all he described. Slowly, purposefully, it began its ascent up her thigh. Each centimeter gained sent ripples of longing coursing through her veins.

"Would you let me lead you into that abyss?" Marcus asked, his fingers dancing ever higher, their heat searing through the fabric of her dress. "To take what I offer and give yourself to the experience?"

Dana's mouth felt dry, her response lodged somewhere between her rapidly beating heart and the lushness of her parted lips. She nodded, unable to find her voice, transfixed by the boldness of his touch and the journey it foretold.

"Good," Marcus whispered, almost to himself. His hand pressed firmer against her thigh, a silent vow of the control he could exert and the ecstasy that awaited. His fingers traced patterns that left her flesh tingling, aching for more than just a hint of pressure.

"Because," he breathed out, his eyes locking onto hers with a predatory glint, "I intend to explore every fantasy you've been afraid to voice, until you're trembling, spent, and utterly mine."

The words were both a caress and a chain, wrapping around her, binding her to this moment, to the burgeoning need that Marcus so expertly stoked. The air between them was thick with the scent of desire, heavy with the weight of unspoken promises and the electric charge of what was yet to come.

ii

MARCUS'S HAND, EMBOLDENED by the silent acquiescence in Dana's wide, glimmering eyes, ventured beneath the soft fabric of her dress. It moved with a reverence for the curves it encountered, fingers tenderly charting the feverish warmth that betrayed her arousal. The subtle brushes against her sensitive skin were deliberate, lingering at the threshold of pleasure, teasing out the shuddering breaths from her lips.

"Tell me," Marcus murmured, each word dripping with the promise of dark delights, "do you feel how each stroke is orchestrated to worship you? To bring forth the symphony of your desire?"

Dana's reply was caught, a captive in her throat, as she clung to his every touch like a lifeline in turbulent seas. His fingers, skilled and knowing, painted invisible lines of fire that seared into her very core, drawing whimpers from a place deep within her.

With each featherlight caress, Marcus spun a narrative of raw passion, detailing the ways he would claim her body and soul. "I will map every inch of you," he whispered, the timbre of his voice a velvet caress against her ears, "with my hands, my mouth, my being—until you forget where you end and I begin."

The slow dance of his fingertips continued, eliciting a fervent yearning that pooled low in her belly. Each explicit image he conjured—the press of his body pinning hers, the firm grip of his hands guiding her movements—wound the threads of Dana's restraint tighter, until she feared they might snap under the tension of her unspoken pleadings.

"Marcus," she finally gasped, her voice laced with the potent cocktail of fear and longing that his expert touch had stirred within her. Her hands reached out, seeking solidity in a world that his words and caresses made tremble.

"Shh," he soothed, even as his fingers traced circles of liquid heat, feeling her swell against his touch. "Patience. Every sensation is a brick in the foundation of what I will build upon you. Trust in me to construct an edifice of ecstasy that will stand the test of time."

In the echoing silence that followed, punctuated only by the sound of their mingled breaths, the depth of her surrender became clear. She was an open book beneath his masterful hands, and he, the author who penned her pleasure with an unwavering hand.

Dana felt a surge of heat at the apex of her thighs, an instinctive rhythm taking hold as her hips rolled against Marcus's hand, the motion born of deep-seated desires. The fabric of her dress bunched between them, a mere whisper of silk that did little to mask the fervor of her body's response. Her breath hitched with each stroke; his fingers painting promises of pleasure on the sensitive canvas of her skin.

"Mmmm, Yes," she breathed, the word a desperate mantra that escaped her lips without conscious thought. Her plea hung in the charged air between them, a silent acknowledgement of the power he wielded with such effortless grace.

Marcus responded not with words but with action. His touch intensified, fingers pressing with a firmness that coaxed a gasp from Dana's parted lips. The slow burn of anticipation transformed under his ministrations, kindling into an inferno of need that threatened to consume her. Marcus traced the curves of Dana's glistening folds with a practiced touch, savoring the subtle movements and textures of her delicate petals. Each stroke was deliberate, showcasing his mastery in the art of pleasure.

"Is this what you want?" His voice was a low rumble that vibrated through her core, stoking the flames higher. The words were simple, but the weight behind them held Dana captive, ensnared by the promise of surrender and the sweet release that hovered just beyond reach.

"Yes," she panted, the admission tearing from her throat as Marcus continued his relentless pursuit of her pleasure. Her body trembled as his fingers expertly stroked her wet desire, pushing her closer and closer to the edge of bliss. She was completely under his control, surrendering to the passion he evoked with every touch. Dana's moans grew louder as she lost herself in the intense sensations coursing through her. She was his willing puppet, responding eagerly to the commanding movements of his skilled hands on her slick folds.

Her body sang with the intensity of her longing, every nerve ending alight with the fire he stoked within her. Marcus had awakened a hunger that had lain dormant, and now it roared to life, demanding satisfaction with a ferocity that mirrored the passion in his eyes. She clung to him, her anchor in the tempest he'd conjured, her moans a melody rising above the symphony of their joined breaths.

Marcus's voice, deep and resonant, wove through the charged atmosphere, a verbal caress as potent as the strokes of his fingers. "I want to taste every inch of you," he murmured, his words painting visions of a pleasure so acute it bordered on pain. "To hear your cries of release echo against the walls."

Each word that dripped like honey from his lips was a siren's call, igniting a deep desire within her that she could not deny. She felt the lock of control within her crack and give way to the primal urge he awakened. Despite his confident facade, there was a raw honesty in his words that exposed their shared vulnerability, creating an intoxicating tension between them.

"Please," she found herself whispering, her voice barely recognizable to her own ears, thick with desire.

Her senses were heightened to the point where each breath Marcus took seemed to synchronize with her own. The brush of his thumb over her most sensitive spot sent a pulse of heat that radiated outward, leaving her skin tingling and her mind reeling. She could feel him exploring her, claiming her as his own, his movements deliberate and sure.

"Marcus..." It was all Dana could muster; her plea interwoven with the ecstasy that coursed through her veins.

In response, his touch grew bolder, more insistent. "Surrender to me," he coaxed, his tone laced with the intoxicating blend of command and seduction. "Let go. I will take you there—to the very edge and beyond."

And she did surrender. Her body arched, a bow pulled taut by the masterful hands of an archer, ready to release its arrow. Her moans filled the space between them, unguarded expressions of the rapture that gripped her. Each sound was a note in the symphony he conducted, a testament to the potency of his touch and the depth of her longing.

The room faded away, the boundaries of her world shrinking until there was only Marcus—the epicenter of her universe. His presence commanded her reality, the power of his touch dictating the rhythm of her heart. In this moment, he was both her anchor and the storm, a paradoxical force that drew her deeper into the tempest of sensation.

Dana's surrender was complete, her spirit soaring on the wings of the pleasure Marcus conjured. She was adrift in the haze, her body moving in time with his provocations, each stroke pushing her closer to the precipice. The anticipation of release hung heavy; an exquisite promise whispered by the man who held her unraveling threads in his capable hands.

iv

Electricity seemed to crackle in the air, a tangible current that pulsed with the rhythm of Dana's quickening heartbeat. The world around them narrowed down to the intimate space they shared, Marcus's fingers the conductors of an exquisite energy that danced across her skin, stirring her senses into a maelstrom of desire.

Her breath hitched, each inhalation mingling with the low, seductive timbre of Marcus's voice as he whispered promises that both soothed and inflamed. "Close your eyes," he coaxed, his words a velvet caress against the shell of her ear. "Feel everything."

Dana obeyed, her eyelids fluttering shut, surrendering to the darkness that heightened every sensation. Marcus's touch was masterful, an artist's brush strokes igniting the canvas of her flesh with colors of passion she'd never known. His fingers traced delicate patterns, mapping the terrain of her longing with a precision that left her gasping.

"Marcus," she breathed out, her voice a quivering thread of sound. It was all she could muster—a single word that conveyed the depth of her need, her utter dependence on the man who expertly navigated the tides of her arousal.

"Shh," he soothed, his other hand cradling her face, thumb gently stroking her cheek. "Let yourself feel it all. I've got you."

The assurance in his grip, the control he wielded over her pleasure—it was intoxicating. With every deliberate movement, Marcus seemed to draw her further from the shore of inhibition, guiding her into uncharted waters where only their joined desires ruled.

Her body trembled, a delicate quiver that started at the core of her being and radiated outward. Each nuance of pressure from Marcus's exploring fingers tipped her closer to the abyss, her anticipation building like a crescendo in a symphony, each note more desperate than the last.

"Good?" Marcus's voice was thick with his own restrained need, the single word reverberating through her.

"Yes," she managed to reply, a plea woven within the affirmation.

There was a silent understanding that passed between them then, a mutual recognition of the power dynamic that thrummed at the heart of their encounter. He, the commanding presence that held her ecstasy in his hands; she, the willing participant aching to be led to the pinnacle of pleasure.

The room contracted, the air charged with the magnetism of their connection, as if the very molecules were rearranging themselves in response to the crescendo of desire that Marcus orchestrated. Dana's senses were so finely tuned to his every motion, every breath, that the rest of the world ceased to exist.

She teetered on the precipice, her body a tightrope walker balancing on the thin line between control and abandonment. And it was Marcus—a maestro of sensation—who would tip her over the edge, into the rapture waiting with open arms.

CHAPTER 6

Steven's gaze was fixated, almost hypnotized by the surreal scene before him on the plush sectional couch. The warm embrace of the ambient lighting accentuated every curve and angle of Dana's body, a captivating play of shadow and light against Marcus's towering figure. His heart pounded erratically; a tumultuous symphony of desire tinged with bitter envy.

Compelled by an impulse to distract his spiraling thoughts, Steven's attention shifted through the haze of sensuality that permeated the club, settling on Thomas. Earlier in the evening, his easy smile and welcoming demeanor had marked him as approachable amidst the sea of enigmatic strangers.

While keeping a watchful eye on his stunning wife, who was lost in her own exploration, Steven made his way through the buzzing crowd, each step echoing his internal turmoil. He finally reached the bar, where Thomas stood alone, emanating a sense of calm that contrasted with the charged energy of the room.

"Thomas, right?" Steven's voice emerged steadier than he felt, offering a hand which was met with a firm, warm grip.

"Indeed," Thomas replied, his smile reaching his eyes, which held a spark of recognition. "And you are?"

"Steven," he responded, acutely aware of how the simple act of introducing himself here held more weight than any previous social nicety.

"First-timer?" Thomas's question, posed with a tilt of the head, was not accusatory but open, inviting Steven into a shared space of candor.

Steven nodded, the admission unlocking something within him. "Yeah... it's all pretty new to me. I'm just trying to get a lay of the land, so to speak." There was a laugh hidden in his words, though it was edged with nerves.

"Understandable," Thomas acknowledged, his tone rich with warmth. "It can be overwhelming, but there's beauty in the chaos, discovery in the unknown."

Their conversation flowed naturally, a counterpoint to the explicit scenes playing out around them. Steven found himself entranced not only by Thomas's words but by the cadence of his speech—the way his voice dipped into husky timbres when he articulated his experiences, suggesting realms of pleasure yet unexplored by Steven.

"Everyone's journey here is unique," Thomas mused, leaning casually against the polished surface of the bar. "But one thing's for sure—you'll never forget your first time."

Steven's pulse quickened at the implication, his mind painting vivid images of what such an inaugural adventure might entail. The allure of the unknown beckoned, seductive and potent, promising a world where desire reigned supreme, and control could be deliciously surrendered or assertively seized.

Thomas caught the glint of curiosity in Steven's eyes and gestured towards a more intimate setting away from the thrum of the club. "Let's find somewhere a bit quieter," he suggested, threading his way through the sea of bodies with an ease that spoke of familiarity.

Steven followed, his senses heightened, each step an exercise in restraint as he navigated the heady atmosphere. They settled into a secluded table with a vantage point that afforded them privacy while allowing the voyeuristic pleasure of observation—a perfect perch to survey the landscape of carnal exploration unfolding before them.

"Comfortable?" Thomas asked, his voice a smooth caress against Steven's growing anticipation.

"Yes, thank you," Steven replied, though a quickened heartbeat betrayed his calm exterior. The soft glow of ambient lighting danced across Thomas's features, casting him in a sensual hue that beckoned Steven closer. He leaned in, driven by an insatiable need to uncover the secrets this man held.

"I've seen things here that have... changed my perspective on what pleasure can be," Thomas started, his tone laced with the weight of experience. "There's a freedom in these walls—a permission to explore without judgment." His gaze never wavered, pinning Steven with a look that invited confession.

"Tell me about it," Steven prompted, his voice barely audible above the crescendo of moans and whispered entreaties around them. The words felt like a key turning in a lock, granting access to a trove of hidden desires.

Thomas shifted, closing the space between them. "It's not just about the physical acts," he murmured, the undercurrents of his voice hinting at deeper pleasures. "It's the connection, the push and pull of dominance and submission, the dance of power and surrender."

Steven's skin prickled with goosebumps, a visceral response to Thomas's proximity and the charged words that painted pictures in the dark canvas of his mind. Here was a man who understood the complex choreography of needs and wants, who moved with grace through the delicate interplay of control.

"Each encounter is an exploration," Thomas continued, his hand grazing the tabletop, fingertips trailing an invisible line that seemed to connect directly to Steven's core. "You learn as much about yourself as you do your partners."

The implication of self-discovery mingled with desire filled Steven with a heady mix of trepidation and longing. In Thomas's narrative, he found a mirror to his own unspoken yearnings, a guide through the labyrinth of flesh and emotion.

"Have you ever surrendered completely, given yourself over to someone else's command?" Steven ventured, the question both a probe into Thomas's experiences and a reflection of his own burgeoning curiosity.

Thomas smiled, a slow spread of lips that promised tales of ecstasy and abandon. "Oh, Steven, the stories I could share..." His voice trailed off, leaving an invitation hanging in the air like the sweetest of scents, drawing Steven deeper into the intoxicating world that lay just beyond the edge of his known universe.

Thomas's voice was a soft caress against the din of the club as he began to unfurl the memory of Lila. "She had this aura, you know? The kind that pulls you in without a single word," he said, his gaze momentarily lost in the recollection. "The night I met her here, it was like we were the only two people in the room."

Steven leaned closer; his glass of whiskey forgotten as Thomas painted the scene. Their knees brushed under the table, an electric jolt at the simple touch. He could almost see Lila through Thomas's eyes—the cascade of brown hair, the piercing blue that promised a world of untold pleasures.

"Her touch was deliberate, intentional. It's as if her fingers spoke a language my skin was aching to understand," Thomas whispered, and Steven felt the words like a stroke against his own flesh. "And when she kissed me..." He paused, letting the moment linger between them. "It was like she was mapping every corner of my soul."

Steven's breath hitched, and he could feel himself being drawn into the intimacy of Thomas's experience. His imagination conjured the taste of such a kiss, the hunger for connection so palpable it bordered on tangible.

"From there, it was an exploration of senses. The scent of her perfume mixed with the warmth of her skin became the only thing I could focus on," Thomas detailed further, describing how they moved together, a dance of desire that left nothing untouched.

"Tell me more," Steven urged, his voice rough around the edges. The need to live vicariously through Thomas's tale was overwhelming, a flame stoked by the embers of his own curiosity.

"Ah, but then there are the other nights," Thomas said with a knowing look, shifting the narrative. "The club offers many paths. Sensual massages where hands roam free, guided by nothing but the intent to pleasure and explore."

Steven swallowed, imagining those hands on his body, strong and sure, pressing away the tension and replacing it with a hunger for more. He shifted in his seat, aware of the growing tightness in his clothes.

"Or the group encounters," Thomas continued, lowering his voice to a conspiratorial hum. "A symphony of moans and sighs, each person both an instrument and a musician. It's an art form, really, the way bodies can move together, separate, then come back as one."

Each word sketched vivid images in Steven's mind, the ebb and flow of intertwined limbs, the cacophony of shared ecstasy. The thought of being part of such a collective experience, of surrendering to the current of collective desire, sent a thrill racing down his spine.

"Control is a curious thing here," Thomas mused. "Sometimes, you wield it; other times, you relinquish it willingly. Either way, you find yourself in the throes of something profound."

"Profound," Steven echoed, feeling the weight and truth of the word. His journey tonight was more than a fleeting adventure; it was a dive into the depths of his own wants, a test of the bonds he held dear.

Thomas raised his glass in a silent toast to the unspoken understanding blooming between them. With each shared secret, each confessed longing, Steven felt less like an outsider and more a part of a world where the lines of fantasy and reality blissfully blurred.

Steven's breath hitched as he leaned closer, the heat of his curiosity mingling with an unfamiliar yearning. "Tell me about Lila," he found himself saying, a mix of reverence and desire lacing his voice. "What was it like... playing with her?"

The corners of Thomas' lips curled into a knowing smile, his eyes shimmering with mischief and memories. With a tilt of his head, he beckoned Steven closer, as if to share a sacred secret between the pulse of music and the whispered confessions that lingered in the air.

"Playing with Lila," Thomas began, his voice a low, velvety caress that seemed to stroke Steven's senses, "it's like dancing on the edge of a blade—thrilling, dangerous, and utterly intoxicating."

Steven felt the room shrink around them, the world outside their conversation fading to a mere backdrop. He watched Thomas' face, observed the subtle shifts of expression, the way his eyes darkened as he recounted his experiences, the raw power of those shared moments hanging palpably between them.

"Once, she took complete control," Thomas continued, the timbre of his voice painting a vivid scene. "She had this look in her eyes—a fierce determination that said she would accept nothing less than my absolute surrender."

Steven could almost see Lila standing before Thomas, her piercing blue gaze commanding and unwavering. The image sent a shiver down his spine, awakening a longing to be under such a spell, to relinquish the reins and trust someone so implicitly.

"Her touch," Thomas said, pausing for effect, "was both a command and a promise. She guided me through a labyrinth of sensation, each move calculated to push me, to expand the limits of what I thought I could feel."

With every word, Steven's imagination unfurled, unveiling a tableau of tactile explorations—soft whispers of fabric against skin, the firm pressure of a binding clasp, the sweet sting of release. It was a dance of dominance and submission, a choreography that required trust as its foundation and yielded pleasure as its reward.

"The beauty of it," Thomas murmured, leaning back and fixing Steven with a look that seemed to see right through him, "was in the letting go. In giving her the reins, I found a strength I didn't know I had—the strength to be vulnerable, to be led to ecstasy by her hand."

Steven swallowed, feeling a resonance within himself, an echo of Thomas' words that rang with truth. There was power in yielding, in trusting another to navigate the complexities of desire. It was a revelation that beckoned to him, tempting him to step beyond the confines of his own boundaries.

"Trust," Steven mused aloud, the concept wrapping around him like a silken thread, binding him to this new insight. And in that moment, amidst the thrumming energy of the club and the intimate tales of passion shared, Steven glimpsed a path to his own exploration—one he never knew he yearned to travel until now.

Steven's heartbeat quickened, a symphony of longing and intrigue set to the rhythm of Thomas' voice. The contours of his fantasies began to take shape, vivid and pliant, influenced by the stories that spilled from Thomas' lips like fine wine—heady and liberating.

"Imagine," Thomas said, drawing a finger through the condensation on his glass, "the thrill of the unknown. Crossing those invisible lines with someone who understands the silence between your words."

Steven pictured Dana, her eyes wide with anticipation, mirroring the hunger in his own gaze. He could feel the air charged around them as they ventured together into uncharted territories of their desires, guided by whispers and shared breaths. It was an intoxicating thought, laced with both trepidation and an insatiable curiosity.

"Trust is the currency here," Thomas continued, breaking into Steven's reverie with a knowing smile. "It's about more than just the physical—it's allowing someone to read the story of your body, word by unspoken word."

"Communication," Steven echoed, feeling the truth of it resonate within him. "Without it, we're just bodies colliding without purpose."

His mind wandered to the conversations he'd had with Dana, the layers of their relationship peeled back to reveal the raw core of their connection.

"Exactly," Thomas agreed, his tone earnest. "You learn to listen with more than your ears. You hear the catch in a breath, the silent plea in a held gaze. And when you respond... when you truly respond, that's where the magic is."

Steven nodded, feeling the camaraderie between them solidify, two men sharing the same revelations. They were kindred spirits in a dance of discovery, each step forward a testament to the bravery it took to be vulnerable with another person.

"Have you ever felt completely seen?" Thomas asked, leaning closer, his voice barely above the music's pulse.

"Seen, and not judged," Steven replied, the concept blooming within him like a nocturnal flower. "To be accepted in that moment, without pretense... it's freeing."

"Ah, freedom," Thomas sighed, a wistful glint in his eye. "The paradox of submitting to another's will, only to find yourself liberated."

In the dim light of the club, surrounded by hushed moans and clandestine encounters, Steven felt the duality of his own nature. The yearning to possess and be possessed, to lead and be led, swirled within him—a delicate balance of power that both intimidated and excited him.

"Here's to finding our liberation," Steven raised his glass, the clink echoing their newfound understanding.

"To trust, communication, and the journey ahead," Thomas replied, their glasses meeting in a toast that sealed their shared pursuit of transcendence.

Steven glanced once more at the sectional couch, where figures entwined in a dance of pleasure and consent. Soon, he thought, Dana and he would weave their own narrative into the fabric of this place, threading their experiences with the vibrant colors of trust and the golden hues of shared desire.

Steven shifted in his chair, the leather cool against his skin, a stark contrast to the warmth radiating from within him. "I've watched Dana tonight," he confessed, his voice threading through the intimate space between them. "And I'm torn. It's like there's a storm inside me—primal jealousy on one side, fierce arousal on the other."

Thomas nodded, his eyes reflecting an understanding that only those who have tasted such fervor could recognize. "It's a dance, Steven. A delicate one at that. Jealousy can consume, or it can fuel desire. It's all about harnessing it, using it to stoke the fire rather than letting it burn everything down."

"Have you ever...?" Steven began, pausing as if testing the weight of his words.

"Been jealous?" Thomas filled in smoothly, a small smile playing on his lips. "Certainly. But in this place, I learned to trust the process. To see my partner's pleasure and know it's part of our exploration, not a detour from it."

Their conversation ebbed and flowed like the rhythmic pulse of the club, their voices a counterpoint to the ambient sighs and whispers around them. Steven absorbed each word, allowing the nuances of Thomas's experiences to color his perception, to shift his view from fear to fascination.

"Trust seems to be the linchpin," Steven mused aloud.

"Indeed," Thomas agreed, his gaze steady. "Without it, we're just ships passing in the night. With it, we're voyagers on the same tumultuous sea, navigating by shared constellations of consent and mutual desire."

Steven felt a kinship with Thomas that went beyond mere conversation. They were two souls cast adrift in the vast ocean of human longing, seeking to understand the currents that propelled them. This recognition wrapped around Steven like a comforting shroud, emboldening him to delve deeper into his psyche.

"Sometimes I wonder if I'm enough," Steven admitted, his voice a whisper against the backdrop of the club's sensual symphony. "If my want to explore is selfish, or if it's part of growing—together with Dana."

"Self-doubt is natural," Thomas said, his tone both reassuring and conspiratorial. "But consider this: your journey is as much about self-discovery as it is about discovering each other anew. The person you are in this moment—with all your desires, fears, and questions—is enough."

As they talked, Steven's notions of power, control, and surrender intermingled, blurring the lines between leading and following. It was as though every confession brought him closer to the essence of his own cravings, his yearning to taste the forbidden fruit of liberation without losing himself in the garden of earthly delights.

"Thank you, Thomas," Steven said sincerely, his eyes mirroring the gratitude that swelled in his chest. "For making me feel seen. Understood."

"Anytime, friend," Thomas replied, clapping Steven on the shoulder with a camaraderie that was both grounding and uplifting. "Remember, you're not alone on this voyage. We're all uncovering the maps to our hidden treasures."

With a deep breath, Steven allowed himself to relax into the newfound solidarity. The tapestry of the evening continued to unfold around them, threads of intimacy and revelation weaving together in a pattern uniquely their own.

CHAPTER 7

The pulse of the club's music faded to a distant throb in Dana's ears as Marcus's aura enveloped her, his proximity an invisible force that pulled at the threads of her self-restraint. His towering presence loomed behind her, a promise of strength and command that made her breath catch in her throat.

"Let go," Marcus whispered, his voice a velvet command that caressed the nape of her neck. "Trust me to lead you where you need to be."

She felt the heat of him against her back, the solid wall of his chest barely touching yet igniting a fire within her. The normally shy Dana found herself nodding, giving silent permission for him to guide her along this new, thrilling path.

His large hand, with fingers that spoke of both gentleness and power, threaded through her long blonde locks, gripping them just firmly enough to tilt her head back. She yielded to the pull, exposing the vulnerable line of her neck to his gaze – and his mouth.

Marcus's lips traced the curve of her throat, his tongue drawing a languid path that contrasted sharply with the slight pinch as he nipped at her delicate skin. The sweet sting sent a rush of adrenaline surging through her veins, mingling with the burgeoning heat of desire.

"Does this please you?" he murmured against her skin, each word vibrating through her flesh like a plucked string.

"Yes," Dana breathed out, the word more an exhalation of surrender than a mere affirmative. Her body was a live wire, every sense heightened by his touch, every thought consumed by the need for more.

The sensation of pleasure laced with pain, so foreign yet so intoxicating, wove through her, binding her to Marcus's will. Her spine arched involuntarily, pressing her against the hardness of his body, seeking something she couldn't yet name but recognized as an essential part of her awakening.

"Good," Marcus said, his approval resonant in the small space between them. "I want you to feel everything. To know that it's me who brings you to these heights."

Dana's response was swallowed by the deepening kiss on her neck, his lips and teeth marking her in a dance of dominance and submission. Each gentle bite, each soothing lick, they were all declarations of his control over her pleasure—a control she willingly, eagerly ceded to him.

Marcus's voice was a low rumble, barely distinguishable from the thumping bass that reverberated through the club's walls. "There's a place where we can be alone," he said, his breath hot against her ear. The suggestion was more command than question, his tone leaving little room for dissent.

Dana's heart hammered in her chest; each beat a drumroll of anticipation. She had never ventured into such uncharted territory, but the thought of being secluded with Marcus, away from prying eyes, sent thrills spiraling through her veins.

"Lead the way," she managed to reply, her voice steadier than she felt.

As they began to navigate through the throng of bodies, Dana sought out Steven. Their eyes met across the crowded room, his gaze heavy with a complex mix of emotions—curiosity, desire, a hint of trepidation. Wordlessly, she beckoned him, an invitation to witness, to join, to be a part of the unfolding journey of their shared exploration.

Steven's response was immediate, a subtle nod before he pushed off the bar and started after them, his presence a silent anchor in the sea of sensory overload.

The private room loomed ahead, a promise of intimacy and revelations, a sanctuary where power dynamics could unfurl in their most intricate patterns.

ii

Marcus's grip was both gentle and commanding as he took Dana's hand, leading her down a dimly lit corridor lined with doors that promised secrets and untold pleasures. The soft carpet beneath their feet muffled their steps, lending an air of privacy to their procession. Each door they passed was like a silent sentinel, guarding the mysteries within.

Dana's pulse quickened, and she could feel the warmth of Marcus's hand seeping into her own—a lifeline as she stepped further away from the world she knew and closer to the brink of something transformative. His touch was a constant reminder of the decision she had made to explore this new realm of desire, with all its risks and rewards.

As they approached the end of the corridor, Marcus paused before a door, turning the handle with deliberate slowness. The click of the latch seemed to echo in Dana's ears, a definitive sound marking the threshold of their adventure. He pushed the door open, revealing a room bathed in the soft glow of ambient lighting that cast everything in a warm, inviting hue.

"Welcome," Marcus said, his voice deep and resonant, a tone that resonated with the very core of her being. His words were few but laden with the promise of what was to come.

Steven entered the room shortly after them, his presence almost ghostlike as he moved through the doorway. Dana felt a flash of heat at the sight of him there—part of this experience, yet apart from it, a witness to the unfolding events. He crossed the room with measured steps, taking up a position at the head of the bed, the fabric of the plush comforter whispering beneath his touch as he sat down. His eyes never left Dana, reflecting a mixture of apprehension and arousal that mirrored her own.

The room felt like a world unto itself, disconnected from the reality beyond its walls. Here, time seemed to slow, each second stretching out, heavy with anticipation.

"Are you ready?" Marcus asked, the simple question loaded with the weight of consent and trust.

She swallowed hard, nodding. "Yes," she whispered, her voice barely audible over the pounding of her heart.

"Good," Marcus replied with a hint of approval. "I want you to let go. Trust me to guide you." His words wound around her, binding her not with ropes but with the power of his intent.

Dana drew a deep breath, feeling the last of her inhibitions begin to dissolve under the intensity of Marcus's gaze. She was here, on the precipice of surrender, ready to give herself over to the exploration of pleasure and power, with her husband as both participant and observer. It was a dance she longed to perform. She felt poised to step into the rhythm of desires yet to be discovered.

ii

In the chamber of whispered secrets and longing, the air hummed with the electricity of unspoken promises. Marcus pressed Dana firmly against the cool wall, its starkness a contrast to the heat emanating from their entwined bodies. His hands mapped the terrain of her curves like an explorer claiming new territory, each touch igniting fires along her skin.

"Let yourself feel everything," Marcus murmured against her lips, his voice a velvet command that caressed her senses. His kiss was an art form, passionate and consuming, speaking the language of desire that left no room for doubt. She could taste the hunger in him, a mirror to her own, as she kissed him back with a fervor that belied her usually reserved nature.

Dana's breath hitched in her throat as Marcus's fingers traced the hem of her dress, venturing beneath it with a boldness that made her heart race. The slow pace of his exploration was maddening, a deliberate tease that had her pushing against him, seeking more. She felt his smile against her neck, a knowing curve of his lips that acknowledged the power he held.

"Patience," he whispered, his breath hot on her skin. "I will take you to heights you've never reached, but you must trust me."

In one fluid movement, he turned her world upside down, flipping her onto her back with a strength that left her breathless. Now on the soft surface of the bed, she gazed up at him, the dim light casting shadows across the planes of his face. His eyes were dark pools of promise, locking onto hers with an intensity that anchored her to the moment.

Marcus positioned himself between her legs, an unspoken claim that resonated deep within her core. His fingertips resumed their dance, now delving deeper, a tantalizing promise of what was to come. Each brush of his touch was more insistent than the last, a crescendo of need that pulsed through her veins.

"Marcus..." Dana's voice broke on his name, the sound a mix of plea and permission that seemed to reverberate through the room.

"Shhh," he soothed, even as his fingers continued their relentless pursuit of her pleasure. "Just feel. I have you."

And she did feel—every stroke, every tease, a symphony of sensation that threatened to overwhelm her. It was a delicate balance, this giving and taking of control, a dance they performed with their bodies and their wills intertwined.

Outside of their cocoon, the world faded into insignificance. Inside, Marcus commanded the tempo of her arousal, guiding her ever closer to the precipice of ecstasy with a mastery that left her utterly at his mercy. And above all, she wanted to fall.

Dana's breath hitched, a crescendo of moans spilling from her lips as Marcus's fingers continued their exquisite torment. The air in the room became thick with the scent of desire, every brush of his touch igniting her senses, as if he was playing her body like a finely tuned instrument. Her hips undulated involuntarily, seeking more of his tantalizing caress, her skin ablaze with an urgent heat that only he could quench.

"Please, Marcus," she gasped, the words tumbling out amidst labored breaths. Her plea was raw, unfiltered by the usual barriers of her shyness. In this space, with him, Dana felt liberated from the confines of her own reticence.

"Patience, my sweet," Marcus murmured, his voice a low rumble that vibrated through her core. "I will take you there, to the edge and beyond."

His hand retreated suddenly, leaving a void that had Dana arching off the cushioned surface in silent protest. But the emptiness was short-lived as Marcus shifted his position, his presence a heavy weight between her thighs. She felt the warmth of his breath against her sensitized flesh. She felt her panties slide off her legs before his mouth connected with her intimately, his tongue delivering a deliberate lick that sent shockwaves rippling through her entire being.

Dana's hands found the edge of the bed, gripping it as though it were her lifeline in the storm of pleasure that Marcus conjured with each flick and swirl of his tongue. Her back arched, pushing her closer to his devouring mouth, surrendering herself to the relentless waves that crashed over her senses.

"Ah, God... Marcus!" she cried, her voice laced with the ecstasy that coursed unchecked through her veins. Every lap of his tongue stoked the fire within her, building, building—until she was teetering on the brink, desperate for release, yet savoring the sweet torture of the ascent.

In the midst of the maelstrom, the power dynamics between them were crystal clear: Marcus was the maestro, conducting her pleasure with masterful strokes, while Dana was the willing instrument, resonating with the symphony of their shared desire. The control he wielded over her was complete, yet it was given freely, a testament to the trust and unspoken understanding that flowed between them.

And Dana, lost in the depths of sensation, realized that this—this unraveling at his hands—was what she had been yearning for all along.

Marcus's relentless pursuit of her pleasure grew more fervent, his tongue tracing intricate patterns that pulled her ever closer to the precipice. Dana's breath hitched, her chest heaving with each gasp as the tension in her body wound tighter, coiling like a spring ready to snap. She could feel every nerve ending alight with an electric charge, the air around them charged with the raw energy of their connection.

"Marcus... please..." she whimpered, her plea barely a whisper, yet laden with the weight of her mounting need.

He responded not with words but with a deepened intensity, his mouth and tongue working in concert to draw out her climax. And then, as if hit by a lightning strike, Dana shattered. Her orgasm thundered through her, a tidal wave of ecstasy that left no part of her untouched. Her voice broke free, uninhibited and raw, calling out his name into the charged silence of the room.

"Marcus!"

Her body convulsed in ripples of unending delight, each wave crashing harder than the last, leaving her adrift in a sea of bliss. Marcus, steadfast in his ministrations, anchored her through the storm, his mouth a constant source of pleasure even as she rode the aftershocks of her release.

Breathless and spent, Dana lay trembling under the weight of what had just transpired, the realization of her own depths of desire dawning on her like a revelation. But there was no time to reflect; Marcus was far from done with her.

With a rough tug, Marcus yanks Dana up to her feet. She gasps for air as he towers over her, his hands moving swiftly to pull her dress over her head and unclasp her bra, leaving her completely vulnerable and exposed before him. Her skin is flushed and radiant, glowing with a sheen of sweat. Her breasts are heaving with each breath, her nipples hard and peaked from his touch. Her hair falls in tangled waves around her face, framing her features in a wild, untamed beauty.

Dana's heart races with a mix of fear and excitement as she meets his intense gaze, knowing she is completely at his mercy.

With a violent shove, Marcus spins her around and forces her onto all fours on the bed. As she meets Steven's wide-eyed gaze, Marcus begins to strip himself down behind her, his movements wild and uncontrolled. She can hear the rustle of fabric and the clink of metal as he readies himself to take what he wants from her. The anticipation and fear build in her chest, making it hard to breathe as she awaits his next move.

Marcus stands tall and proud, his chocolate skin glistening in the dim light of the room. Every inch of his muscular body is defined, the result of hours spent at the gym. Beads of sweat cling to his chest, highlighting the curves and ridges of his toned muscles. His stunningly dark cock stands at attention, a symbol of his virility and strength.

In contrast, Dana's body exudes softness and femininity. Her creamy white skin glows against the dark backdrop, her curves a gentle invitation to be explored. Together, they are a perfect juxtaposition - yin and yang, light and dark, hard and soft.

Without warning, he shifts the tone of their encounter, his rough hands roaming with newfound urgency. He grips her long golden hair, pulling her head back to expose the column of her throat, his lips branding a trail of fiery kisses down her skin. The sound of their breathing becomes heavier as Marcus positions himself behind Dana, the anticipation and intensity of the moment increasing with each passing second. As he enters her from behind, their moans and gasps mingle, creating a symphony of pleasure.

As Marcus pushes into Dana, she is overwhelmed by the sheer size and power of him. With each forceful entry, he stretches her open like a rag doll and fills her completely, sending waves of intense pleasure through her body. Her senses are consumed by the overwhelming force of their primal connection, as if they are two powerful beasts locked in a relentless battle of desire.

His powerful thrusts pound into her with unyielding force, sending waves of pleasure rippling through her body. Her hair is yanked back so hard it feels like her scalp might tear, but the pain only intensifies the pleasure coursing through her veins. Her full breasts heave and sway in rhythm with his relentless movements, begging for more as she moans and gasps in ecstasy.

Marcus's hand connected with the smooth skin of her backside, the sound echoing loudly in the room before fading into a lingering presence. Each strike leaving behind a stinging sensation, causing her skin to tingle and burn in response. She couldn't help but let out a gasp with each impact, her body betraying her control over the involuntary response to his touch.

"You like that, don't you?" Marcus growled, his voice dripping with both power and desire.

She struggled to form a coherent response, her senses overwhelmed by the intoxicating mix of pain and pleasure coursing through her. As his hand came down once again, leaving behind yet another fiery imprint on her already red skin, she could feel herself surrendering completely to his dominant will.

Dana feels a surge of something wild within her, a fierce joy in the surrender to Marcus's dominant and commanding touch. She couldn't help but arch her back and push back against him as he brought her closer and closer to the edge of ecstasy. The sound of their skin slapping together mixed with their heavy breathing filled the room, creating an intense and primal atmosphere.

"Oh God," she breathed, the words a talisman against any lingering shyness, an embrace of the power she held even in submission.

They moved together, two bodies entwined in a dance of carnal exploration, each touch a discovery, each movement a revelation. Marcus guided her, his hands mapping the contours of her flesh, claiming every inch as his canvas. With each thrust, Dana found a new aspect of herself reflected in the mirror of their passion, a woman reborn in the crucible of their shared lust.

iii

DANA'S EYES WIDENED as she looked up at Steven, her lips parted and her breath coming in short gasps. Her face was a mix of pleasure, pain, and desire, her body trembling with ecstasy as Marcus continued his assault on remains of her defenses.

"More," she urged him, her voice a husky echo of the insatiable craving that drove them onward. And Marcus obliged, pushing her, pushing himself, to explore the furthest reaches of their desires. The room became a world unto itself, where only their pleasure existed, where the boundaries of what Dana had thought possible were redrawn with each gasp, each moan, and each cry that fell from her lips.

Steven's jaw clenches as he watches helplessly, his face contorted with a mix of overwhelming arousal, desperate longing, and deep concern for the love of his life. She is being mercilessly used before his very eyes, her body nothing more than a plaything for another's pleasure. Every nerve in Steven's body screams to rush to her rescue, but he can only sit there, consumed by a maelstrom of conflicting emotions.

Dana's body was on fire, every inch of her skin alive with sensation as Marcus expertly moved within her. She surrendered herself to his touch, losing herself in the primal pleasure that coursed through her veins.

"You want this?" Marcus growls, his hands already pulling her towards the bed.

"Yes," she gasps, her voice thick with desire.

With a primal desire burning within him, he flips her over and roughly throws her onto the soft silk sheets of the bed. His strong hands grip her waist with unyielding force as he pins her down, his eyes blazing with an intense hunger. She eagerly responds, wrapping her legs around him and pulling him closer, their bodies entwining in a tangled mess of lust and yearning. Their passionate embrace is filled with urgent kisses, desperate touches, and heated whispers as they become one in a frenzy of desire and ecstasy.

Their moans and cries fill the room as he thrusts into her with such force that the headboard slams against the wall.

"You like it rough, don't you?" he asks, a hint of amusement in his voice.

She nods, unable to form words as their movements become more primal and frenzied. Their power dynamics constantly shift and intensify, pushing them both towards the edge of ecstasy.

With a deep, primal grunt, Marcus thrusts his hips forward, driving himself into her with force. He grips her thighs tightly, holding them open and allowing him to delve deeper into her depths. Each movement sends a wave of pleasure coursing through her body, tingling and sparking in all the right places. As their bodies move together in perfect rhythm, she feels completely consumed by his touch and lost in the sensation of their intimate connection.

Marcus towers over her, his voice booming with a primal hunger. "Get on top of me," he demands, his eyes burning with lust and dominance. "Prove to me how much you crave my cock." His intense gaze never wavers as he waits for her to fulfill their insatiable desires.

She opens her eyes to see Steven still watching them from his seat on the corner of the bed. His eyes dark with desire and something else that she couldn't quite place. Was it anger? Jealousy?

But before Dana could dwell on it further, Marcus's movements became more urgent and she was once again lost in a haze of ecstasy.

Dana's body trembled with desire as she climbed on top of Marcus, his eyes burning into hers with a mix of intensity and challenge. She could feel his hardness pressing against her, his arousal matching her own.

Without hesitation, Dana slides down onto him, taking him deep inside her. Her body arches and trembles with pleasure as they move together, their bodies finding a primal rhythm that only intensifies their hunger for each other.

Steven's heart races as he watches the scene unfold before him. His love is surrendering to another man's desires, but it only serves to fuel his own desire for her. He can see the raw passion on their faces, the unbridled need in their movements. And even though it causes a pang of jealousy in his chest, he cannot deny the undeniable thrill that courses through him as he bears witness to their passionate union.

As Dana rides Marcus with abandon, she glances over at Steven, locking eyes with him for a brief moment before immersing herself completely in the intense pleasure that Marcus is providing her. She can feel every inch of him inside her, filling her in ways she had never experienced before.

Marcus' hands grip her hips firmly as he thrusts up into her again and again. "You're mine," he growls possessively. And in this moment, Dana doesn't care about anything else but the wild ecstasy that consumes them both.

She moves faster and harder on top of him, driven by an insatiable desire that threatens to consume them both. And Marcus meets every one of her movements with equal fervor until they are both teetering on the brink of release.

She gasped as his strong hands gripped her hips, pulling her closer to him.

"Faster," she moaned, meeting his every thrust with equal urgency. "Yes," he growled, losing himself in the intensity of their coupling. As they reached the peak together, he whispered her name and she cried out.

With one final powerful thrust from Marcus, they both reach their peak together amidst a flurry of screams and moans that echo throughout the room. A surge of ecstasy engulfs them like a raging tempest, threatening to drown them in its powerful embrace. With desperate cries of "Oh God!" and body-shaking gasps, Dana rides the storm of pleasure as Marcus unleashes himself inside her with primal force. Their bodies collide and meld together in the throes of passion, a potent mix of desire and release that leaves them trembling and breathless

Dana collapses onto the bed beside Marcus, their chests heaving as they caught their breaths. For a few moments, there was only silence between them as they basked in the aftermath of their shared pleasure.

CHAPTER 8

Steven's gaze lingered, tracing the contours of Dana's surrendered form, as a knot of desire twisted in his belly. He felt the constriction, an almost painful tightness against the fabric of his trousers, growing with each stolen breath. The air around him seemed to thrum with electricity, charged by the spectacle before his eyes.

He watched – no, he devoured the scene with a hunger that shocked him, a primal urgency that crackled beneath his skin. The sight of Dana, so open and uninhibited, sent waves of heat coursing through him, each pulse echoing the rhythm of his throbbing heart.

Yet amidst this surge of arousal, there was a gnawing sensation clawing at his chest, a specter of jealousy that tainted the sweetness of his longing. Steven grappled with the duality of his emotions, the unspoken question hanging heavy in the room: did his pleasure stem from her exploration, or from his voyeuristic perch?

"Can I truly accept this?" he murmured under his breath, his voice barely audible over the soundscape of soft sighs and whispers of flesh against flesh. His own place in Dana's sphere of desire seemed blurred, undefined, leaving him adrift in a sea of turbulent yearning.

Dana gasped for air, her body trembling with a mixture of pleasure and guilt. She turned toward Steven, their eyes meeting in a fiery gaze. "Is this what you wanted?" she hissed, her voice dripping with a dangerous blend of desire and defiance. Her words cut through the thick haze of arousal that clouded their senses, a reminder of their reckless journey together, their shared pact to push the limits of their passion to the brink.

Steven's response lodged in his throat, a silent testament to the war raging within. He yearned to taste the power of control again, yet the relinquishing of it, the surrender to this complex portrait of desire, held a seductive allure all its own.

She moved in ways that spoke directly to the core of him, every arch and gasp a siren song to his innermost cravings. And as he teetered on the precipice between torment and ecstasy, Steven understood that the path they had chosen was not one of simplicity but of intricate, raw intensity.

"Yes," he finally whispered, his voice a ragged thread of sound. "Yes, that is what I wanted."

With those words, Steven acknowledged the depth of their exploration, the intricate dance of trust and desire. And though the storm of jealousy still brewed within, he sensed the burgeoning warmth of something transformative – an intimacy that defied convention, a connection that promised to reshape the very essence of their union.

Marcus, like a sculptor knowing exactly where to touch, had hands that seemed to mold Dana's curvaceous form, guiding her movements with an authority that both unnerved and captivated Steven. Those strong, dark fingers pressed into the soft flesh of Dana's hips, an ownership in their touch that sparked an exquisite lance of jealousy through Steven.

Dana herself was a study in sensual contrasts. Her blonde hair cascaded over her shoulders, a pale silken curtain swaying with each arch of her back. The vulnerability in that delicate gesture clashed with the fierce abandon she displayed, whilst her body responded to Marcus's guiding hands with a primal rhythm.

The sight was a visceral punch to Steven's senses, heightening every emotion that wrestled within him. It was like watching a dance choreographed by raw desire itself, a testament to human connection free from restraint. And as much as it pained him, Steven could not tear his gaze away. There was beauty in the surrender, an artistry in the way Dana yielded to the moment.

"Incredible," he heard himself murmur, the word slipping out on a breath tinged with awe and edged with a pain that seemed to cut right to his soul. Yet even as the word left him, Steven wondered if he spoke of Dana's flushed appearance or the hauntingly erotic narrative they created.

Muscles tensed to the point of trembling; Steven felt caught in the gravitational pull of the scene unfolding before him. He was adrift in a sea of conflicting currents, each wave of emotion crashing over him with more force than the last. Anticipation for what he knew would come next laced tightly with anxiety for the unknown paths their journey might take.

"God, you move so well together," he whispered, voice barely audible above the symphony of sighs and the subtle music of the club that filled the room. There was no denying the harmony in their movement; Marcus and Dana were two parts of a whole that Steven longed to understand, to be part of, yet also feared losing himself to.

In the shadowed corners of the dimly lit room, amidst the faint scent of musk and the warmth enveloping him, Steven realized that this was a crossing of thresholds. A step beyond the familiar landscape of their love into uncharted territories marked by the pulse of skin against skin, by the silent language of bodies in motion. And in that moment, despite the tempest inside, there was an undeniable truth taking root in his heart: this was transformation, this was revelation, and it was irrevocably theirs to claim.

Steven's heart hammered against his chest, a relentless drumbeat that echoed the tumult within. He watched, almost disembodied, as Dana surrendered to the rhythm of another's guidance. The sight before him was a parade of desire and complexity, threads of power dynamics weaving through the fabric of their union.

The room seemed to contract with each rise and fall of their entwined forms, the air thick with the scent of their exertion. Steven felt the tension coil in the depths of his stomach, an exquisite knot that tightened with every whispered moan that escaped Dana's lips. Her pleasure, raw and uninhibited, acted as both a balm and a flame to Steven's psyche.

Marcus's silhouette moved with assured grace, a conductor orchestrating a symphony of sighs and gasps from Dana. And Steven, witnessing this intimate ballet of flesh, found beauty in the surrender, in the acceptance of his own complex desires.

He could see the silent language of consent in Dana's eyes, the way her body melded to Marcus's touch as if she were clay being sculpted by knowing hands. It was a dance of trust, of exploration, and Steven felt his soul stretch and grow in understanding with every pulse and thrust.

As the crescendo built, Steven's breath hitched, his entire being focused on the connection unfolding before him. There was a sacredness here, in the shared vulnerability, in the silent acknowledgment that they were forever altered by this brazen act of passion.

Finally, as the encounter ebbed, Steven exhaled a long, slow breath he hadn't realized he'd been holding. His muscles unclenched one by one, the tension seeping out of him like sand through open fingers. In the aftermath, quietude wrapped around them like a gentle shroud.

He knew, as he looked upon Dana's flushed face and saw the satiated glow in her eyes, that they had traversed a boundary together, even as she had crossed it with another. This was a new intimacy, a new facet of their love that glimmered with the potential of unexplored depths.

"Mmmm, did you enjoy that dear?" Dana's voice reached out, soft and tentative, yet underscored with a strength that only such openness could forge.

"Very much so," Steven responded, his voice steady despite the tremors that still whispered through him.

In her nod, in the warmth of her gaze, Steven found a sanctuary. They had ventured into the unknown, and what they found there was not division, but a bridge—built of sighs and whispers, of relinquished control and embraced desires—a bridge that promised to carry them to new horizons, together.

CHAPTER 9

With the heat of Marcus's touch still lingering on her skin like the ghost of a sultry whisper, Dana withdrew, inch by increment, from the cocoon of their shared warmth. The room seemed to tilt and sway as she steadied herself, her pulse thrumming in her ears—a testament to the fervor that had just unfolded between them. Amber light glinted off her dewy skin, casting a soft glow that outlined her curvy silhouette.

Marcus stood up from the tousled bed, his lean frame casting a shadow over Dana's breathless form. His dark eyes gleamed mischievously as he gazed down at her.

"Satisfied with what you found?" he playfully inquired, his voice low and seductive.

Dana simply cooed in response, her body still trembling with pleasure. "Yes," she whispered, her cheeks flushed and her hair a wild mess. "Thank you for guiding me," she added, grateful for the moments of ecstasy he had shown her. The room was filled with the musky scent of their passion, a lingering reminder of their intimate encounter.

Marcus gathered his scattered clothes, casting a quick glance over at Steven who sat on the edge of the bed. With a grateful nod, Marcus slipped out of the room, immediately enveloped in a refreshing breeze that provided relief from the stifling heat and his own perspiration. A smile spread across his face as he navigated through the lively and loud atmosphere of the club.

Dana closed her eyes briefly, savoring the memory of how Marcus had navigated the contours of her body with a masterful blend of strength and tenderness. Her breath came in unsteady cascades, each exhale mingling with the charged air of the club. In this moment, Dana felt as though she straddled two worlds—the safety of the familiar and the heady thrill of the unknown.

"Amazing, isn't it?" The voice cut through Dana's reverie, tender yet edged with mischief.

Dana's eyes fluttered open to find Lila standing in front of her. The door to the room stood open. She had no idea how long Lila had been there or how much she'd watched. Marcus had vanished, as if he were a thief in the night who had successfully stolen his prize and disappeared without a trace.

The knowing smile playing on Lila's lips suggested a camaraderie that transcended mere acquaintance. It was the smile of someone who had walked the path Dana now found herself navigating, someone who understood the delicate dance of liberation and vulnerability.

"Was it everything you hoped for?" Lila asked, her tone imbued with genuine curiosity and encouragement. Her piercing blue eyes searched Dana's, seeking not just an answer but an understanding of the journey Dana had embarked upon.

The question hung in the air, a bridge between the two women, inviting Dana to cross into a realm of candid confession and shared secrets. With the remnants of passion still echoing through her being, Dana grappled with the words to encapsulate the tempest of sensation and emotion that Marcus had awakened within her.

Dana's gaze locked with Lila's, the air between them thick with unspoken understanding. "It was... incredible," she began, her voice a whisper of silken sheets against bare skin. "The way Marcus moved, the assertiveness in his touch—it was like he knew exactly what I wanted, what I needed, before I even did."

"Tell me more," Lila urged gently, leaning in closer, her presence enveloping Dana in warmth and acceptance.

"His hands," Dana continued, her pulse quickening at the memory, "they were firm yet so incredibly gentle. It was as if he was sculpting my pleasure from the very air around us, molding it to our wills." She paused; her cheeks flushed with a rosy tint of desire. "But it's also so new, so different from anything I've ever felt. I'm exhilarated, yet I can't shake this tremor of uncertainty within me."

Lila's nod was slow and deliberate, her eyes reflecting the flickering lights of the club as they held Dana's gaze. "That's the beauty of this place," Lila spoke with a voice that wrapped around Dana like a comforting shawl. "The intensity, the exploration—it can be transformative. You're not alone in those feelings, trust me."

"Really?" Dana's question was barely audible, a feather drifting on the edge of doubt.

"Absolutely," Lila affirmed, reaching out to rest a hand lightly on Dana's shoulder. "Everyone here has been where you are now. We've all navigated the torrents of passion and come out the other side knowing ourselves a bit better."

She gave Dana's shoulder a reassuring squeeze. "Your desires, your experiences—they're valid. They're normal and celebrated here. This is a place without judgement, where control can be surrendered safely, and power dynamics play out with mutual respect."

Dana let out a breath she hadn't realized she'd been holding, the tension in her shoulders easing under Lila's touch. The labyrinth of her emotions didn't seem quite so daunting with Lila's words lighting the path.

"Thank you, Lila," she murmured, a tentative smile beginning to bloom on her lips. "I think I needed to hear that."

"Anytime," Lila smiled back, her blue eyes sparkling with an unspoken promise of camaraderie and shared adventure. "We're all on this journey together."

Lila's gaze lingered on Dana, a playful glint emerging in her piercing blue eyes. "You know," she began with a cadence that hummed with suggestion, "there's an entirely different kind of thrill waiting for you and Steven, if you're both daring enough to embrace it."

Dana felt the air grow thick around her, each word from Lila weaving a tantalizing possibility into the fabric of the night. Her chest rose and fell with a rhythm that betrayed her escalating heartbeat as she considered the implication behind Lila's words.

"Thomas and I... we could show you. Together." Lila's voice dropped to a whisper, conspiratorial yet laced with an undeniable excitement. "Imagine the exploration, the heights of pleasure you can reach with not just one set of hands, but many."

As the invitation danced before her, Dana's heart performed a somersault, its beat a chaotic symphony echoing through her veins.

Her eyes shifted across the room to where Steven stood, meticulously gathering her dress and delicate lingerie that had been strewn about during her passionate encounter. Yet, how would he respond to this new, uncharted proposition? Hell, did she even have the energy left to entertain the idea?

Her mind spun with visions of tangled limbs and shared breaths, the thought of surrendering to a collective desire under Steven's steady gaze. Would he find exhilaration in the sight of her unfurling beneath another's touch, or would the green monster of jealousy rear its head within him?

"Isn't it... overwhelming?" Dana's question, barely a whisper, sought affirmation in the midst of her internal maelstrom.

"Overwhelming? Sometimes." Lila's smile was tender, acknowledging the vulnerability in Dana's tone. "But it's also liberating. To be seen, to be wanted by more than one... it's empowering, and when done with care, it can strengthen the bond you already have."

The word 'liberating' hung between them like an offered key, unlocking doors within Dana's psyche she hadn't realized were closed.

The notion of being cradled within a network of trust and lust was intoxicating, a siren call to the part of her that yearned to cast off the shackles of convention.

"Think about it," Lila coaxed gently, her own longing for connection and adventure a silken thread tying their understanding together. "No pressure, just possibilities."

Dana's breath hitched, her skin prickling at the precipice of decision. Could she step beyond the edge, hand in hand with Steven, and plunge into this sea of sensation they were only beginning to navigate? The weight of choice was hers to bear, yet the promise of discovery, of shared power and relinquished control, beckoned with a compelling allure.

"Thank you, Lila," Dana managed, her voice a blend of gratitude and newfound curiosity. "I'll think about it, I really will."

"Of course," Lila responded with a knowing nod. "Whatever you decide, it's your journey. And it's beautiful, no matter the path you choose."

Dana's eyes met Steven's across the room once more, feeling the silent question pulsate through the charged air. Would they dare to explore this seductive terrain together? Only time, and the courage of their desires, would tell.

Lila's fingers were a whisper against Dana's arm, a soothing touch that seemed to anchor her amidst the storm of trepidation and yearning. "Dana," she began, her voice a velvet caress in the dimly lit expanse of the club, "this place... it's about exploration, about finding new edges and gently pushing past them. It's always okay to take a moment, to talk, to ponder."

Dana found her gaze lingering on Lila's lips, the way they curved with empathy, with a deep understanding of the tumult that churned within her. "It's essential," Lila continued, "to communicate openly. Everything here is built upon consent. Speak with Steven; it's a conversation worth having, regardless of where it leads."

The air around them felt thick with unspoken words, heavy with the gravity of what was being offered. Dana drew in a breath, its depth reaching into the core of her being, stirring the embers of curiosity that had begun to glow fiercer within her. She realized then that this was more than an invitation; it was a gateway to the uncharted realms of her own desires.

"Thank you, Lila," Dana murmured, the words ripe with the juices of a ripening courage. Her heart thrummed a primal rhythm, urging her forward as she turned away from the comfort of understanding and toward the uncertainty of growth.

ii

Dana's steps were measured, each one an assertion of her resolve as she navigated across the room to where Steven was waiting with her clothes.

His presence was an unwavering force, one that had always drawn her back from the precipice of her fears. Now, it was time to see if that same force could propel them both into the embrace of the unknown.

She spoke with a mixture of determination and vulnerability, her voice quivering with urgency and adrenaline. "Steven," she said, trying to remain steady but her intensity evident, "Are you okay?"

"I'm fine," Steven replied, concern laced in his tone. "But what about you? That was a lot to handle."

"I'll be fine," she responded with a fierce determination, "I just need a moment to catch my breath."

Dana's fingers, trembling with the weight of unspoken words, grazed Steven's arm. His skin, warm beneath her touch, seemed to pulse with an energy that echoed her own restless heart. She leaned in, her breath a whisper against the cacophony of the club's sensual symphony.

CHAPTER 10

The pulsating rhythm of their heartbeats seemed to sync with the muffled beats of music seeping through the walls of the private room. Dana's skin was still warm, a rosy flush painting her cheeks as Steven's arm, strong and reassuring, wrapped around her waist, pulling her closer into his embrace. The air around them was thick with the remnants of desire, every breath they took laced with the electric charge of their recent tryst.

Steven's gaze, heavy with a cocktail of lust and something far more profound, locked onto Dana's. His pupils were dilated, dark oceans that swirled with an intensity that spoke volumes without a single word uttered. With the gentleness of a feather drifting to the ground, his fingertips traced the line of Dana's jaw, a tender touch that contrasted with the raw passion they had just experienced.

"Are you sure you're okay?" he asked, his voice barely above a whisper, yet it cut through the silence with the strength of a vow. His thumb brushed against her lower lip, a reminder of the kisses they shared, of the promises made without utterance.

Dana's reply was caught in her throat, her emotions a tempest that both frightened and exhilarated her. She nodded, her eyes never leaving his, allowing the silent communication between them to convey what words could not.

In the dim lighting of the room, Steven's face was a canvas of devotion, each feature etched with a story of their love. He leaned in, his breath warm against her ear, and whispered the reaffirmations that tethered them beyond the physical realm. "I love you, Dana. Nothing will ever change that. We're in this together, remember?"

As his words wrapped around her like a protective shroud, Dana felt the steel of their bond, unyielding and steadfast. It was a connection that had weathered storms and basked in sunlight, growing stronger with each new horizon they explored together. With every beat of their hearts and every shared glance, Dana knew that whatever lay ahead, they would face it united, their love the compass guiding them through the vastness of their desires.

Dana's skin hummed with the remnants of ecstasy, a physical echo of Marcus' touch that rippled through her. Yet amid the flickers of pleasure, a profound warmth burgeoned within her chest—one that radiated from the very core of her being. She turned to Steven, her eyes tracing the contours of his face, so familiar and yet endlessly mesmerizing. In this secluded room where whispers of temptation lingered in the air, she found a sanctuary in his gaze.

"Thank you," she breathed out, the words infused with a weight of meaning only they could understand. Dana's gratitude was not merely for the shared carnal adventures but for the unspoken trust that had flourished between them—a trust that had become the bedrock of their exploration into realms untamed by the constraints of conventional love.

Steven, ever attuned to the subtle language of her body, recognized the shimmer of emotion in her eyes. He cupped her cheeks gently, his thumbs stroking the softness of her skin with reverence. The moment hung suspended, a single heartbeat stretched into eternity, before he dipped his head to capture her lips with his own.

The kiss was a silent sonnet, a tender merging of souls that spoke volumes more than any spoken declaration. With each gentle press of his mouth against hers, Steven reaffirmed their unity, the promise that every step they took on this path of desire would be taken together.

Their shared experiences—their trials, their triumphs—were locked within the embrace of this kiss, a symbol of an unbreakable vow.

As she kissed him back, Dana surrendered to the sensation, allowing it to wash over her in waves of passion and tenderness. In the serenity of their connection, she understood that this journey was not about seeking something missing, but rather celebrating the depth of what they already possessed. Together.

Dana's breath caught as Steven's kiss deepened, a tender flame kindling in her chest and spreading warmth through her veins. Her lips moved with his in a slow, deliberate rhythm, the dance of their desires weaving a tapestry of shared devotion. She wrapped her arms around his neck, pulling him closer, her fingers tangling in the soft locks of his hair. Each gentle suckle, each caress of their tongues was a silent affirmation of their love, echoing through their intertwined bodies.

As they parted, a breathless whisper of air filled the space between them, carrying with it the weight of all they had experienced together. Dana's eyes fluttered open to find Steven watching her, his gaze intense and full of purpose. There was no need for words; their hearts spoke a language that transcended speech.

Steven's hands, those sculptors of pleasure, began their descent down the curve of her spine, sending shivers cascading over her skin. His touch was both familiar and exhilarating, every stroke imbued with a promise of more—more love, more passion, more life shared and savored. He traced the contour of her hips, his fingers firm yet gentle, a physical expression of his determination to cherish her, to honor the trust she placed in him.

With each glide of his hand, Steven etched a path of desire on Dana's flesh, a map of the journey they were on together. His fingertips whispered over her thighs, igniting fires of anticipation in their wake. She felt his resolve in every touch, knew that he was reaffirming their bond with every caress. Their love was a fortress against any storm, a testament to the strength they found in each other's embrace.

Dana arched into his touch, her body speaking its own language of yearning. Together, they danced on the edge of ecstasy, each movement a step deeper into the world they had dared to explore—a world where their love proved to be the most exhilarating adventure of all.

ii

A ripple of heat unfurled within Dana as Steven's touch became a silent vow, a pledge of devotion that beckoned her to relinquish all inhibitions. Her breath hitched, a testament to the potent mix of trust and desire that Steven elicited with each deliberate caress. She yearned to be his canvas, to be painted with the colors of their love and lust in bold strokes that would mark her soul and body alike.

"Come back to me," he murmured, his voice a velvet command that coaxed her defenses to crumble. The timbre of dominance laced with the softness of care was a melody that resonated deep within her, a siren song calling her to the depths of shared ecstasy. His words were like sparks against dry tinder, an ignition for the smoldering want that had nestled within her core.

"Steven..." Dana's whisper was both a plea and a declaration, her eyes reflecting the flames that his whispers had stoked. She was ready to dive into the abyss of pleasure he promised, to wrap herself in the safety of his arms while they ventured into the unknown together.

His lips grazed the shell of her ear, sending a shudder through her. "I need you, Dana. Every part of you." His words danced down her neck, leaving a trail of goosebumps in their wake. "Every inch of your skin is a path I long to explore, a journey I want to take over and over again."

His breath, hot against her skin, drew a path to her collarbone, each word punctuated by a kiss that sealed their covenant. "And I will always be here, to cherish you, to protect you," he continued, his hands anchoring her to the present, to the reality of their boundless connection.

Dana surrendered to the tide of passion Steven evoked, her body an instrument played expertly by his hands. His promise enveloped her, a tangible testament to the depths of their bond. Here, in the cocoon of their desire, she felt invincible—buoyed by the strength of his words, the certainty of his love. Together, they would soar, transcending the ordinary and touching the divine.

Dana's breath hitched as Steven's hands charted unseen maps across her skin. The room around them faded, its edges blurring into insignificance as his fingers traced the rise and fall of her curves with a reverence that spoke volumes. She could feel the tension coil within her, an exquisite anticipation that made every stroke, every caress a promise of what was to come.

He guided her gently, with a certainty that whispered of countless nights spent learning the language of her body—a dialect of sighs and whispers, a grammar of touches and glances. They moved together in a rhythm as old as time, yet as fresh and thrilling as the first drop of rain on parched earth. With each movement, they delved deeper into a shared realm of sensation, a world where only they existed, bound by the intensity of their union.

Steven's touch was deliberate, the controlled strength of his hands contrasting with the gentle way he kissed her, as if each brush of his lips was both a question and an answer. He navigated the contours of her pleasure, steering them through the waves with the skill of a masterful captain, attuned to the silent communication between their bodies.

The ebb and flow of their passion built a crescendo that left Dana teetering on the brink of ecstasy, her senses alight with the fire of his ministrations. Each kiss was a pledge, each touch a testament to the bond they had forged—a bond not even the wildest tempests could rend asunder. In the sanctuary of Steven's embrace, she found herself pushing past boundaries she once held sacred, discovering new territories of delight within her soul.

As Steven's movements became a symphony of desire and control, Dana felt herself surrender to the rhythm, her body an instrument that sang under his deft direction. The edge of ecstasy loomed close, a precipice that promised the sweetest of falls. With every breath, with every beat of her heart, she soared higher, buoyed by the strength of their connection, until at last, they reached the pinnacle—a place where love and passion collided in perfect harmony.

Dana's breath came in short gasps, each one a silent anthem of her newfound liberation. She was adrift in an ocean of sensation, each wave crashing over her with the force of revelation. Steven's touch had become the compass by which she navigated this uncharted expanse of desire—a desire that was all at once hers alone and theirs together.

Beneath the weight of his gaze, something within her unfurled like a flower daring to bloom in the wild. There was no shame here, only the raw beauty of her fantasies taking flight, lifted on the updraft of their mutual exploration. Dana's heart swelled with empowerment, her mind awash with the knowledge that each whispered secret, each shared craving, had become the bedrock upon which they built their temple of intimacy.

Across the space that hummed with their shared energy, Steven watched her with eyes alight with pride. There was no conquering here, only the witnessing of Dana's metamorphosis, where her surrender was not a yielding but a triumphant ascent into the vastness of their passion. He felt it then, the surge of love that transcended physical bounds, a pulsing connection that wove through them, stitching their souls together in a tapestry rich with the colors of trust and acceptance.

"Beautiful," he breathed, the word more a benediction than a mere compliment, and Dana knew he spoke not just of her form, but of the essence of her being laid bare before him.

Their journey—fraught with the dangers of the unknown, laced with the thrill of discovery—had led them here. To this moment where Steven's steady presence was the anchor in Dana's tempest of release, and her unguarded passion was the beacon guiding him home. Together, they danced on the edge of eternity, every movement a declaration, every sigh a promise that the depths of their passion were as boundless as the night sky above.

A ripple of ecstasy surged through Dana, her breath catching in the hollow of her throat as waves of pleasure cascaded over her. Steven's arms were a fortress around her, his rhythm unyielding yet profoundly attuned to every quiver that shook her frame. Their gaze locked—a mirror of souls laid bare—they soared, crests of passion lifting them higher until, in a burst of shared release, they shattered into a million stars.

In the aftermath, their bodies remained entwined, a living testament to the voyage they had embarked upon together. Steven's chest heaved against Dana's back, his heartbeat a drumming echo to hers. Gradually, their breathing synchronized, a gentle ebb and flow that cradled them in its soothing rhythm.

"Steven," she whispered, her voice a tender thread in the quietude of the room. The sound of her name on her lips was a beacon, guiding him back from the edge of transcendence.

He tightened his embrace, a silent vow encompassing every fiber of his being. Tenderly, he brushed a strand of hair from her damp forehead, his fingers trailing along her jawline with a reverence that spoke volumes. Their intimacy was not merely physical; it was a fusion of spirit, a melding of hearts that no force could rend asunder.

With care, Steven shifted, drawing Dana into his lap. She nestled against his chest, the solid warmth of him a balm to the tremors that still danced beneath her skin. His hands, those instruments of ardor, now glided over her with a gentleness that belied the fervor of moments ago. Each touch reaffirmed their bond, each kiss a seal upon the promise of forever.

"Look at us," he murmured, his voice a low thrum that vibrated against her ear. "Stronger than ever." It was more than words; it was an incantation, imbuing them with the power of their shared odyssey.

Dana lifted her eyes to meet his, and in that exchange, they found affirmation. They had traversed landscapes of desire and faced the tempests of doubt, only to discover that within each other lay an infinite reservoir of strength. Here in this sanctuary, they had woven a tapestry of trust, painted with the hues of their deepest passions and hung upon the framework of their devotion.

As they basked in the afterglow, the world outside faded to a distant murmur. Nothing else mattered but the truth that resided in the space between their two hearts—the certainty that together, they were invincible.

"Steven," she murmured, her voice laced with a gravity that belied the sultry atmosphere, "can we go somewhere and talk? There's something... I need to share with you."

Her eyes searched his for a sign of understanding, a flicker of recognition at the undercurrents swirling between them. Steven's gaze held hers, dark pools reflecting the myriad of neon lights, yet somehow deeper, promising the thrill of uncharted depths.

"Of course," he replied, his voice a resonant timbre that threaded through her senses. He stood, offering his hand, a silent vow to stand by her side as they navigated the tides of desire and trepidation.

CHAPTER 11

With the chamber of her carnal secrets left behind, they moved through the thrumming heart of the club, past entwined figures that danced on the edges of restraint. The dimly lit corridor stretched before them, a path to seclusion that promised intimacy and revelation. Dana's heels clicked against the polished floor, a staccato beat that matched the racing of her pulse.

Steven guided her to a corner veiled in shadows, where plush velvet couches offered a sanctuary amidst the tempest of sensuality. He sat, his posture relaxed, yet every line of his body attuned to her presence. She settled beside him, close enough to feel the heat radiating from his form, their thighs nearly brushing in the semi-darkness.

"Steven," she began anew, her voice a caress that sought to bridge the distance fear had imposed. Her fingers found his, intertwining with a tender boldness that anchored her. "There's something Lila suggested—"

The words hung in the air, a delicate invitation to step beyond the familiar into a realm of shared discovery. Her breath hitched, anticipation knotting within her as she awaited his response, ready to unfurl the secrets of her longing under his attentive gaze.

Dana's breath drew deep, the air quivering in her chest like a harp string plucked by tentative fingers. She turned toward Steven, her lashes casting a shadow over eyes alight with the flicker of inner turmoil and yearning.

"Steven," she whispered, her voice threading through the hush that cloaked their private alcove. "Lila—she proposed something... intriguing." The word trailed off, caressed by the velvet touch of possibility.

She watched his face, the subtle interplay of light and darkness across his features. Her heart swelled, caught between the precipice of fear and the abyss of desire. Each beat was a drumroll to her confession, as she unfurled the ribbon of Lila's suggestion before him.

"It's about us," Dana continued, each syllable heavy with the weight of uncharted longing. "About expanding the horizons of what we share, exploring together. It's... it's an invitation to join them, Lila and Thomas."

The silence stretched between them like a canvas awaiting the artist's first stroke. Steven's gaze never wavered, his attention a testament to the gravity of her revelation. His dark eyes, usually so assertive, now danced with reflections of her own complex emotions.

"Imagine it, love," she said, her voice barely above a murmur, yet resonant with the tremor of excitement. "The chance to delve into depths unknown, to taste the fruit of shared fantasies. To learn, to grow, to trust even more deeply than we have."

Each word was a brushstroke on the canvas of their relationship, painting in hues of passion and curiosity. She offered her desires up to him, a tender sacrifice upon the altar of their bond.

Steven remained still for a heartbeat, two, allowing the waves of implication to wash over him. Then, with a motion as deliberate as the tide, he reached out. His hand encased hers, warm and reassuring, the lines of his palm pressing against the softness of her skin.

His touch was a silent covenant, a nonverbal echo of the sentiments she laid bare. In the simple act of intertwining fingers, he spoke volumes. Yes, to the venture into sensuality. Yes, to the vulnerability inherent in their exploration. Yes, to her, to them, to the future painted in shades of pleasure and mutual discovery.

"If you really feel you're okay and you really think you're up for it," he breathed, the words a velvet balm that sealed their silent accord. In the quietude of their sequestered nook, amidst the distant echoes of carnal delight, Steven and Dana sat united, hands clasped, spirits entwined, on the cusp of a new dawn in their odyssey of desire.

"We didn't come all this way just to sit around and rest," she playfully retorted. "This is our chance to explore, to seize the unknown and make it ours. Tomorrow may never come, but this opportunity is right in front of us now." Her eyes glittered with determination as she spoke, daring anyone to stand in their way.

"No matter what, I'll be by your side. If you want to continue exploring, then that's exactly what we'll do," he assured her.

ii

Rising from the velvet cocoon that had cradled their intimate exchange, Dana felt a ripple of excitement surge through her as she stood. Their fingers remained entwined, anchoring each other in the midst of swirling anticipation. It was as though they were two adventurers at the threshold of an uncharted realm, hearts drumming the rhythm of newfound daring.

Steven's gaze met hers, a silent conversation flowing between them. His eyes, once clouded with uncertainty, now shimmered with the same fervent spark that ignited within her. In that moment, it was as if they had discovered a secret language, their shared understanding transcending words, their connection deepened by the promise of mutual exploration.

They navigated through the club's labyrinthine pathways, a mingling of shadows and whispers guiding them back to where Lila and Thomas awaited. With each step, the air grew thick with the electricity of potential, the very atmosphere charged with the tantalizing pulse of what could be.

Dana caught Steven's eye again, the intensity of his dark irises reflecting her own desires back at her—a mirror of passion yet to be unfurled. The corners of his lips quirked upwards, a silent tribute to the trust that swathed them like a second skin. Their movement towards Lila and Thomas felt ceremonial, each stride a testament to the decision that unified them.

"Are we really doing this?" Steven's voice was a low murmur, for her ears only, vibrating with the undercurrents of exhilaration.

Dana squeezed his hand, her own voice a whispering caress against the din of the club. "Yes, together," she affirmed, her words laced with the potency of shared fantasies and a future painted in bold strokes of intimacy and mutual surrender.

As they approached Lila and Thomas, the couple turned to greet them, their expressions etched with the knowingness of those who had long since danced along the delicate edge of desire. Thomas's easygoing smile was a beacon of encouragement, while Lila's blue eyes glittered with the allure of adventures untold.

"Ready?" Lila's question hung in the air; a gentle challenge wrapped in the velvet of her voice.

Dana felt Steven's hand tighten around hers, a silent harbinger of the pact they had forged. She nodded; the gesture imbued with the weight of their joint resolve. "We are," she said, her voice steady yet humming with the vibrant pulse of their decision.

In the space between them, the air seemed to hum with the resonance of consent, the four individuals encircled by the invisible threads of anticipation and the unspoken agreement to venture into the depths of pleasure and connection—together.

iii

The quartet nestled into the velvety confines of a semi-private lounge; each pair perched on opposite ends of a crescent-shaped sofa that seemed to embrace their shared anticipation. Lila crossed her legs, the movement sinuous and deliberate, as she leaned forward, her fingers tracing abstract patterns on the low glass table between them.

"Let's talk about what you both want," she began, her voice a sultry tune that resonated with the promise of untapped desires.

"Boundaries are sacred here," Thomas interjected softly, his words an anchor in the sea of burgeoning excitement. "Whatever you're comfortable with, we honor."

Dana felt the heat rise in her cheeks, yet she found a strength in her vulnerability. She glanced at Steven, seeking reassurance in the steady gaze he offered back, before turning to address Lila and Thomas. "We've talked about this," Dana started, her tone laced with the thrill of confession. "We're curious about... sharing, but we need to go at our own pace."

"Of course," Lila murmured, her nod slow, encouraging. "It's about exploring together, finding what heightens the pleasure for all of us."

Steven shifted, his posture opening up as he entered the exchange. "We like the idea of watching and being watched to start," he said, firm yet curious, his hand subtly squeezing Dana's thigh under the concealment of shadows.

"Watching can be its own kind of touch," Thomas agreed, his voice a velvet rumble that seemed to stroke the air around them.

"Consent is the key that unlocks all doors here," Lila added, her gaze locked with Dana's, blue eyes shimmering with the depth of oceans yet to be charted. "And communication—it's the map that guides us."

Dana nodded, feeling the taut string of nerves within her loosen ever so slightly at the affirmation of her agency. "Yes, communication. We'll speak up if something doesn't feel right," she asserted, the weight of her own words grounding her.

"Perfect," Lila said with a soft clap of her hands, the sound a gentle punctuation in their cocoon of conversation. "Let's start there then. This evening, let's indulge in the art of observation. We'll remain attuned to each other's cues."

"After we watch, we are comfortable with Dana playing with both of you. She has no rules to follow from me however I do not engage in intercourse with anyone other than Dana," Steven offered, "Does that work for you both?"

"Yes, that suits us just fine," Thomas declared, his smile an easy curve that held the night's secrets.

They continued to converse, the dialogue ebbing and flowing like the tide, washing over details and nuances, crafting an understanding that felt as intimate as the touch they contemplated. In the sanctuary of shared expectations, Dana's pulse thrummed with the rhythm of discovery, each beat an echo of the power dynamics they willingly wove into the tapestry of their connection.

As the discussion drew to a close, they stood, their bodies drawing near in silent assent. The walk back to the heart of the club was a procession of mutual consent, every step a dance of desire and control, a prelude to the symphony of sensuality that awaited them.

CHAPTER 12

The click of the door, as it sealed shut behind them, seemed to resonate through Dana's very core. In the dimly lit sanctum, shadows danced along the walls, playing with the soft contours of her anticipation-swollen cheeks. The murmur of the club outside was muffled now, a distant echo compared to the muffled tunes that caressed the air within, wrapping around the four of them like a silk scarf, light and sensuous.

"Welcome to our little escape," Lila's voice was honey over gravel, smooth with an edge of excitement as she turned, her piercing blue eyes locking onto Dana's with an intensity that sent a shiver down her spine. Dana's breath caught in her throat, her curvy figure rigid with a nervous energy that tingled on her skin.

"Let's not keep desire waiting," Lila whispered, her gaze never wavering from Dana's. With a grace that belied her eager pulse, Lila sauntered towards the bed that dominated the room, beckoning the others to follow with a crook of her finger.

Steven's hand found Dana's, his fingers lacing with hers, squeezing gently—a lifeline amidst the torrent of emotions that threatened to sweep her away. She could feel his arousal in the tension of his grip, the subtle tremor that spoke of his own battle with jealousy and yearning.

"Shall we?" Thomas's voice was a velvet rumble, close enough that Dana could detect the undercurrent of his own desires, his lean build poised on the cusp of action, ready to dive into the depths of the night's promises.

Lila reached the edge of the plush bed and paused, her back an elegant line that commanded attention. "Clothes are merely barriers," she said, her tone a mix of command and seduction. "Let us rid ourselves of such constraints."

One by one, they obeyed, garments slipping from bodies like leaves falling from autumn trees—slowly at first, then all at once. Dana watched, her heart thudding in her chest, as Lila's dress pooled at her feet, revealing the confident lines of her body. Steven's shirt came next, the fabric whispering to the floor, exposing the tautness of his chest that spoke of quiet strength.

Dana felt her own hands moving almost as if they belonged to someone else, unbuttoning, unzipping, until the cool air caressed her bare skin, goosebumps erupting across her flesh. Her clothes joined the others', a tangle of discarded inhibitions that lay forgotten as the reality of their vulnerability set in.

"Beautiful," Lila murmured,

Dana stood confidently in front of Lila,

Dana's nude body was a masterpiece on display, perfect in every curve and muscle. The soft lighting caressed her toned arms and slender legs, while casting shadows over her alluring curves. Lila's eyes roamed over every inch of her smooth skin, unable to resist the raw sensuality that emanated from her. The air in the room was charged with tension as Dana stood confidently, her nakedness a challenge for Lila to resist its seductive power.

"Come," Lila beckoned again, this time her voice softer, a feather drifting through the tense atmosphere. Her invitation was more than words—it was the opening verse to a song of sensuality they were about to compose together, note by heated note.

As the distance closed between them, the bed became their anchor in the storm of passion that loomed on the horizon, each movement deliberate, each breath a shared cadence in the symphony of the night that awaited.

ii

The mattress dipped softly under their collective weight, the plush surface cradling Dana as she found herself nestled between Steven's solid frame and the lithe silhouette of Thomas.

Lila reclined in front of them, bare body a landscape of curves and valleys, the soft light casting shadows across her skin, emphasizing the gentle slopes of her hips and the rise of her breasts. Her curves are accentuated by the soft lighting in the room, casting shadows over her toned muscles and shapely legs. Her confident posture exuding a boldness that can't be ignored. An enigmatic smile danced on her lips, her piercing blue eyes glimmering with a mischievous knowledge.

The air was thick with tension, every breath they took seemed to weave them tighter into this web of intimate potential.

"Let's not rush," Lila's voice was a purr, her gaze holding each of theirs in turn. "Explore... feel every sensation." Her suggestion lingered in the air like a fine mist, seeping into their consciousness, guiding their actions.

Dana's pulse quickened; her skin already sensitized to the mere suggestion of contact. She felt the gentle warmth of Steven's thigh against hers, the accidental brush sending a shiver down her spine. Across from her, Thomas' chest rose and fell with a steadiness that belied his own burgeoning excitement.

Thomas, lean and toned, with defined muscles rippling beneath the smooth skin. His shoulders are broad and his chest is sculpted, with small patches of dark hair contrasting against his pale skin. As her gaze travels down his body, Dana can see that his stomach is flat and toned, leading to a tantalizing V-shape at his hips. His legs are long and muscular, each movement displaying strength and agility. And between his legs, his erection stands thick and proud, the head glistening with excitement. She could sense the heat emanating from his body, even from a distance.

Slowly, almost reverently, Dana extended a trembling hand towards Steven, her fingertips grazing the landscape of his skin. The ridges of his muscles danced under her touch, eliciting from him a soft groan that vibrated through the quiet room. His dark eyes, heavy with desire, met hers, and she read in them an encouragement that propelled her forward.

Beside her, Thomas mirrored her movement, reaching out with a tentative boldness that spoke of his easygoing nature. His fingers traced an invisible line along Lila's arm, drawing from her a delighted sigh that sounded like a hymn to the night's promises.

The cacophony of the club beyond the walls faded further into obscurity as soft moans began to punctuate the silence, the soundtrack of their exploration. Each touch, each caress, unfolded layers of anticipation, building a languid rhythm that pulsed through the dimly lit chamber.

Steven's hand found Dana's, their fingers intertwining, a silent pact of mutual surrender to the experience. Her other hand wandered, emboldened by Lila's encouraging nods, over the curve of Thomas's shoulder, feeling the tautness of his skin beneath her palm.

Lila leaned in, her movements fluid and confident, and whispered into the charged space between them, "Close your eyes, let go of everything but what you feel."

As Dana closed her eyes and let go of all her inhibitions, she was transported to a world where everything was fluid and uncertain. She could feel the heat emanating from Steven's body as he pressed closer to her, his hands exploring every inch of her skin with a delicate yet insistent touch.

Thomas' fingers danced along Lila's curves, tracing patterns of longing and desire onto her skin. The two women moaned in unison, their bodies responding to the other's touch as if they were one entity.

With each passing moment, Dana felt herself letting go more and more, succumbing to the sensuality of the moment. Her mind was blissfully blank, all thoughts pushed aside by the overwhelming sensations coursing through her body.

As Steven's lips brushed against hers, Dana opened her mouth eagerly, their tongues entwining in a dance as old as time itself. She could taste both his desire and hers on his lips, a heady mixture that only fueled their passion further.

Beside them, Thomas' lips trailed down Lila's neck, leaving a trail of hot kisses in their wake. He took his time exploring her body with an almost reverent touch, each caress drawing out delightful moans from Lila.

Dana could feel herself getting lost in the intensity of it all as Steven's hands ran up and down her back, igniting sparks of pleasure with every touch. Their bodies moved together in perfect harmony as if they had been dancing this dance forever.

In this timeless space, they surrendered to the unfolding narrative of their joined bodies, each chapter written with a kiss, a caress, a gasp. Here, in the sanctuary of shadows and whispers, they composed a symphony of sensuality, each note resonating with the deep thrum of primal instincts and the delicate harmony of newfound trust.

iii

Dana's fingertips danced across Steven's chest, tracing the hard lines of his muscles with a featherlight touch that belied her trembling desire. The softness of his skin beneath her hands sent ripples of heat coursing through her veins, and she marveled at the contrast between his strength and the vulnerability they now shared in this intimate haven.

Their gazes locked, and for a moment, Dana was lost in the depths of Steven's eyes—dark pools of unspoken promises and simmering passions. She leaned forward, her lips finding his in an urgent, impassioned kiss that spoke volumes of their shared yearning. Their tongues met, twining together in a languid dance that mirrored the ache within her—a rhythm as old as time yet as fresh as the first drop of rain on parched earth.

As desire wound its way around them like a silken thread, pulling them into its embrace, they became voyeurs to the sensuality unfolding beside them. Lila, with the grace of a feline predator, moved with deliberate intent, her body a symphony of curves and whispers against the canvas of the bed. Each sway of her hips was a call, a siren song to which Thomas responded with a hunger that was both primal and tender.

Thomas's hand glided over the expanse of Lila's thigh; a journey of exploration marked by the shiver that traveled up her spine. His fingers were artists, and her skin was the masterpiece upon which he composed his affections. When his lips finally claimed hers, it was not just a kiss—it was an assertion of desire, a silent declaration that here, in this realm of flesh and shadows, they were equals in their surrender.

Dana felt a surge of something powerful within her—a mix of arousal and revelation—as she witnessed the interplay of dominance and submission, the fluid exchange of control between Lila and Thomas. It was a dance she and Steven were only beginning to understand, each step forward a leap into the unknown realms of their own desires.

The power in the room shifted, ebbing and flowing like a living thing. Dana's breath hitched as Lila's hand extended toward her, an unspoken invitation that pulsed with promise. Dana rose to meet her, the soft carpet beneath her feet now forgotten as she stepped into the embrace of possibility.

"Come here," Lila coaxed, her voice a velvet caress that wrapped around Dana's soul. With a glance that held all the secrets of the night, Dana obeyed, her movements deliberate yet hesitant, a deer stepping into an enchanted glen.

Thomas watched her approach, his eyes dark pools of silent encouragement. As Dana neared, he reached out, his touch gentle on her waist, guiding her down beside him with reverent ease. There was an implicit understanding in his grip—a knowledge that he was there to both lead and support her in this journey.

Thomas leaned in close, his hot breath tickling Dana's ear as he whispered soothing words. Her body quivered at his touch, electric sensations coursing through her. His skilled hands moved across her skin with a grace and precision, mapping every curve and dip with care. Dana gave herself over to his touch, surrendering to the waves of pleasure that he expertly coaxed from her. Each gentle caress felt like a masterpiece being crafted by a master artist, every motion deliberate and purposeful. In this moment, she was lost in the depths of passion and desire, guided by Thomas' skilled hands and mesmerizing presence.

Steven, from his vantage point, observed the unfolding scene with a complexity of emotions. Desire bloomed within him, hot and insistent, as he watched Lila join them on the bed, her presence a magnetic force. She turned her attention to Dana, her gaze holding a spark of mischief.

"May I?" Lila asked, her tone laced with both respect and yearning. Dana's nod was shy, but her eyes were alive with desire.

Lila leaned in close, her lips a whisper away from Dana's delicate skin. She traced a path of soft kisses along the curve of her neck, each one a gentle exploration that set off sparks and ignited a tiny flame within Dana. With every tender bite, meticulously measured and placed, Lila stoked the fires higher, creating a map of sensation that left Dana gasping for air. Steven's heart raced in his chest, pounding like thunder at the sight of his wife blossoming under Lila's touch. Her body trembled with pleasure, her breath coming in short gasps as she surrendered to the electric current running through her body.

"Beautiful," Lila murmured, her words barely audible over the crescendo of Dana's quickening breaths. There was a reverence in how she handled Dana, a silent vow to cherish the trust bestowed upon her in this sacred space of discovery.

Steven felt the stirrings of something deeper than physical want—an emotional tide that swept through him, mingling pride with a vulnerability he had never dared acknowledge before. He was entranced by Dana's unfolding, by the way she gave herself over to the experiences, her usual inhibitions replaced by a hunger that mirrored his own.

Dana's eyes were closed, her face an expression of bliss as she surrendered to the sensations coursing through her body.

Lila's delicate fingers, soft and graceful, traced over each curve of her skin with practiced ease. Thomas' arms, strong and chiseled, encircled her in a gentle but firm embrace, holding her close as they swayed to the rhythm of their own love song. Each touch and movement was a dance, a symphony of passion and tenderness. Their bodies moved in perfect harmony, like two puzzle pieces fitting together flawlessly. In that moment, nothing else existed except for the warmth of their embrace and the intoxicating scent of desire filling the air.

In this charged atmosphere, where only their interwoven desires existed, Dana, Steven, Thomas, and Lila found themselves not just crossing boundaries but redrawing them together, crafting a tapestry of pleasure that would forever hang in the gallery of their intertwined souls.

iv

Dana's breath hitched as Lila's fingers traced a path along her thigh, the coolness of her touch contrasting with the warmth that bloomed beneath her skin. Thomas's hands, assertive and knowing, roamed with gentle authority over the curves that Steven had always worshipped in private. Now, they were an offering to new deities of desire within the dimly lit sanctuary of this room.

"Let yourself feel," Thomas whispered into Dana's ear, his voice a velvet command that coaxed her deeper into the labyrinth of sensation.

And she did. She let go completely, every breath a willing sacrifice to the ecstasy that enveloped her from four pairs of hands, each touch like a binding spell tightening her to this journey of sensual discovery.

Lila's skilled tongue explored every inch of Dana's quivering body, igniting an inferno of pleasure within her. The intoxicating heat radiating between their entwined bodies only fueled their desire as Lila expertly licked and teased Dana's sensitive flesh with a fervent passion. Moans and sighs escaped Dana's lips in a symphony of bliss, each touch sending shivers down her spine. Lost in the throes of ecstasy, she surrendered herself completely to Lila, allowing her to consume her with unbridled devotion.

The bed became their altar, their movements ritualistic as they indulged in the divinity of flesh. With each shift, each repositioning, the dynamics of power subtly transformed, a fluid dance where leading and yielding were as natural as breathing. Thomas, entwined with Dana, dominated the space with a tender ferocity that left her grasping for moorings in the tempest of her arousal.

"Exquisite," Lila murmured again, her gaze locked on the couple before her, her own body a conduit of pleasure as she weaved in and out of their embrace, amplifying every sensation.

The air grew dense, saturated with the essence of their arousal, the music of their shared ecstasy rising in volume. Moans became a chorus, punctuated by gasps that kept time with the rhythmic collision of skin against skin. The scent of sex was heavy, a tangible presence that mingled with the sounds of their symphony, each note struck on the chords of their bodies a testament to the heights they scaled together.

"More," Dana panted, the word torn from her throat as much a plea as it was an affirmation of her own hunger. The power she once held in reserve now fully unleashed, fueling the flames that danced across her skin with every touch, every kiss.

"Always more," came Lila's response, her breath a warm breeze against Dana's fevered flesh. Her words were both a promise and a benediction, spoken by one who knew the contours of these peaks well, who had scaled them countless times and still revered their majesty.

Together, they crested waves of passion, their cries intermingling, becoming indistinguishable as individual desires melded into a single, pulsating entity. And within that entity, Dana found a freedom that only comes from complete surrender—a surrender to the moment, to the others, to the overwhelming tide of pleasure that threatened to sweep them all away.

Steven's breath fanned across Dana's skin, a tactile whisper that spoke to the fervor mounting within him. He leaned in, his lips tracing the curvature of her neck with reverence, before claiming her mouth in a kiss that was both affirmation and initiation. The taste of her, a mixture of sweet and salt, roused him to action—a call to join the symphony of their shared pleasure.

His hands, once tentative, now moved with purpose, molding to the contours of her hips as he entered her. Dana arched against him, her sighs spilling into the air, each one a note in their carnal composition. Steven, feeling the pulse of her desire, found his own mirrored there. This was more than physical; it was an exploration of depths previously undiscovered, a journey they embarked upon together.

As Steven moved inside Dana, he felt Thomas' gaze upon him like a starving predator, ready to pounce. His eyes burned with an electric intensity, filled with ownership and desire that could not be ignored. Thomas's presence was palpable, radiating off of him in waves that sent shivers down Steven's spine. Every move, every touch, was tinged with the weight of Thomas's watchful stare. It was both thrilling and unnerving, making Steven feel like nothing more than prey in the face of such predatory hunger.

"Let me," Thomas' voice rumbled low, a deep and primal sound that echoed through the air. It reached out to Steven, carrying with it an undercurrent of shared understanding. In this moment, they were connected in ways beyond physical pleasure; their desires and boundaries blurred as they surrendered to each other.

In this space, no possession was absolute; they were fluid, shifting like tides beneath the moon's pull. Their bodies intertwined in a dance of passion and trust. It was a sacred union between three souls, bound by love and desire.

Steven relinquished his place to Thomas with a nod, an unspoken trust passing between them. He watched, a silent guardian, as Thomas took over, entering Dana with a careful assertiveness that seemed to draw forth even deeper moans from her. The sight of her beneath Thomas—her body yielding, seeking, demanding—stirred something primal within Steven.

Dana's world narrowed to the sensation of Thomas inside her—the stretch and fill, the perfect friction. Her nerves sang, alight with the sting of Thomas's firm hand as it caressed her flesh, pushing her closer to the edge of an abyss she yearned to tumble into.

"Is this what you want?" Thomas's question was both a taunt and an offering, his voice threaded with dark promise.

"More," she breathed, her voice breaking on the word—a testament to the intensity of her need.

Steven, stirred by the scene unfolding before him, felt the stirrings of a possessive ache blend with the joy of witnessing Dana's abandon. He moved closer, his body intertwining with hers and Lila's, whose lips traced a path along Dana's collarbone. Their movements became a dance of desire, each touch a declaration, every gasp a surrender to the collective ecstasy they built together.

"Give yourself to this moment," Lila whispered, her words tinged with the wisdom of one who had surrendered many times and found strength in vulnerability.

Dana surrendered to the rhythmic waves of pleasure, her body undulating in response to Thomas' movements inside her as Steven's lips once again captured hers in a passionate kiss. The three of them were intertwined, each person a master and vessel of their own pleasure, lost in a labyrinth of sensation. Together, they explored the unknown depths of desire, solidifying their bond with every movement and touch.

The room was electric with their connection, every caress a spark, every thrust a surge, their desires colliding, merging, transforming into a power that none could wield alone. They were at once masters and disciples of their passion, learning the language of each other's bodies, writing their story upon the canvas of flushed skin and tangled limbs.

In this realm, where control ebbed and flowed, they discovered unity—an equilibrium where power dynamics bowed to the greater force of their joined hunger. Each exchange of dominance and submission was a conversation spoken not in words but in the language of touch, a dialect of sighs and moans that only those who have traversed these intimate landscapes can truly comprehend.

Here, in this consecrated space, they redefined the boundaries of their intimacy, etching new lines upon the map of their union, venturing into territories marked by the bold signature of their shared desire.

v

The crescendo of their shared ecstasy loomed on the horizon, a tempestuous sea of passion that promised to engulf them all. Dana's senses were ablaze as Steven and Thomas, two forces of nature, danced upon the precipice of control with her body as their canvas. Lila's caresses painted strokes of fire across her skin, each touch igniting another spark in the tinderbox of desire they had built together.

"Let go," Steven's voice was a velvet command in Dana's ear, his breath hot against her neck—his presence an anchor in the maelstrom of sensation that threatened to sweep her away. She looked into his eyes, dark pools of intense love and raw desire that reflected her own tumultuous emotions.

Thomas, with the deft precision of a maestro, conducted the rhythm of their pleasure—a symphony of flesh and longing that resonated through Dana's core. The world contracted until there was nothing but the bed, their entwined bodies, and the acute focus of nerve endings singing with impending release.

"More," Dana whispered, a single word that conveyed the depth of her need. Her voice was both plea and permission, a surrender to the exquisite tension that pulled taut between them.

"Always more for you," Thomas replied, his words punctuated by the fervent movements that drove them ever closer to the edge.

Their cries began to echo off the walls, a chorus of carnal delight that melded into one unified expression of rapture. Dana felt herself spiraling, caught up in the whirlwind of hands, lips, and the relentless push and pull of bodies chasing the ultimate peak.

And then it crashed over them, a tidal wave of pure, blinding pleasure that washed away thought and time, leaving only the pulsing beat of hearts and the shuddering release of pent-up desire. They cried out, a quartet of voices harmonizing in the throes of climax, the sound a testament to the power they wielded together.

As the last tremors of ecstasy ebbed, the intensity that had fueled them subsided into a gentle glow of satisfaction. They collapsed into a tangled heap of limbs and contented sighs, the warmth of skin on skin a comforting embrace that held the echoes of their shared bliss.

Steven drew Dana close, his arms encircling her in a protective cocoon as she nestled against his chest. Their sweat-dampened skin merged, a silent language of intimacy that spoke volumes of the trust and connection they had deepened this night. Lila and Thomas lay beside them, their presence a soothing balm to the embers of passion that still flickered within.

"Beautiful," Lila murmured, her voice a soft melody that seemed to vibrate with the residual energy of the room.

"Amazing," Thomas agreed, his hand finding Steven's in a gesture of camaraderie and shared understanding.

In the aftermath, they lingered in the sanctuary of each other's arms, their breathing slowly returning to normal. The silence was profound, not for lack of words, but because it was filled with the weight of an experience that transcended language—the indelible mark of a journey taken together, one that would forever alter the landscape of their desires.

vi

Dana's eyelids fluttered open, the world returning in soft focus as she lay entangled amidst a sea of contentment. The gentle rise and fall of Steven's chest beneath her cheek was a rhythmic anchor, a tender reminder of the love they shared and the boundaries they had pushed together. His fingers combed slowly through her blonde tresses, trailing paths of warmth that whispered promises of forever.

"Thank you," she breathed out, the words barely a sigh against his skin. Her senses were still awash with the scent of musk and the echo of pleasure that resonated in the quiet room.

"Every moment... a discovery," Steven replied, his voice a deep murmur that vibrated through Dana's very core, igniting a smoldering wick of desire that hadn't quite extinguished.

Beside them, Lila's arm draped over both Dana and Thomas, her fingertips dancing lightly across their intertwined hands. Her eyes shone with the luminescence of shared secrets, her smile a silent ode to the escapades that had unfolded. "We've taken an incredible journey together," she said, her tone infused with reverence for the intricate patterns of intimacy they'd created.

Thomas, whose presence had been a steady force of encouragement, nodded in agreement. "More than flesh joined; it's our spirits that have mingled." His hand squeezed Dana's gently, acknowledging the trust and surrender that had painted their collective canvas with strokes of bold exploration.

The afterglow bathed them in its golden light, bringing into relief the contours of their bodies, the slight sheen of their satisfaction. In this cocoon, the power dynamics that had once seemed so defined now flowed like water—fluid, changing, and harmonious.

"Changed," Dana whispered again, her voice gaining strength as she absorbed the magnitude of what had transpired. A shiver of vulnerability trailed down her spine, but it was quickly soothed by the circle of acceptance surrounding her.

"Empowered," Lila added, her piercing blue eyes reflecting a fierce pride that echoed in the depths of Dana's soul.

"Connected," Thomas concluded, as if he had unveiled a profound truth that stretched beyond the confines of the bed they occupied.

The room held them in its embrace, the shadows cast by the dim light playing across their forms. Time seemed to stretch, languid and indulgent, allowing them to savor the lingering touches, the soft exchanges, the quiet understanding that bloomed in the silence.

In this space, where passion had raged and settled into tenderness, Dana found herself cradled not just by her husband, but by a newfound family forged in the fires of desire and quenched in the waters of mutual respect.

"Forever altered," Steven intoned softly, encapsulating the sentiment that pulsed through each of them.

"Forever," Dana agreed, her heart swelling with the knowledge that they had embraced the unknown and emerged not only unscathed but enriched, emboldened, and profoundly connected.

CHAPTER 13

The door to the private room closed behind them with a hushed click, sealing away the secret heat of their encounter. Dana's heart was still racing, her skin tingling and warm as if Steven's caress lingered upon her flesh. She felt every strand of her long, blonde hair brush against her back with each step, a sensual reminder of the abandon she had just experienced.

They ventured through the softly lit maze of the club, their interlocked fingers a lifeline anchoring them to reality after soaring through the stratosphere of pleasure. The dim lighting cast shadows that danced along the walls, mirroring the flame of contentment that flickered between them.

Steven, his dark hair slightly tousled, exuded a quiet confidence that had always drawn Dana to him. His touch was gentle yet firm, guiding her through the labyrinth with an assuredness that spoke of deeper layers in their relationship—layers they were only just beginning to uncover.

"Are you okay?" Steven's voice was soft, a tender note that vibrated through the charged air between them.

Dana's reply was a whisper, her words wrapped in the warmth of her breath. "More than okay," she said, her voice steady despite the whirlwind of emotions swirling within her. Her shyness, once a cloak she wrapped tightly around herself, now hung loose and open, revealing a boldness that surprised even her.

Their pace slowed, not out of necessity, but from a desire to prolong this interlude between worlds—their private sanctuary of fulfillment and the vast unknown that awaited outside the club's walls. Each step seemed to mark the rhythm of their newfound connection, the echoes of their footsteps a metronome to the pulse of their shared exhilaration.

"Tonight was...incredible," Steven confessed, his words laced with the gravity of their adventure, the thrill of the unknown that had enticed and tested him.

Dana squeezed his hand, the gesture intimate and full of meaning. They had crossed lines together, explored the terrain of their desires, and found solace in each other's bravery. And as they reached for the handle of the exit, the cool anticipation of the night beyond beckoned them forward—a silent promise that the exploration of their depths was only just beginning.

ii

Dana's hand was a gentle anchor in Steven's as they navigated the shadowy maze that twisted through the club. The muted throb of music grew fainter with every step they took toward the exit, replaced by the soft sighs and murmurs that danced upon the heavy air. Around them, the silhouettes of others were caught in the throes of passion, each scene a testament to the raw desires that unified all within these walls.

The sensual glow of red and amber lights kissed the contours of bodies entwined, casting a warm hue on skin glistening with exertion and abandon. Dana's gaze traced the curve of a spine arched in ecstasy, the clasp of hands locked in fervent need, and she felt a resonance within her own flesh - an echo of the pleasure she had just surrendered to.

Steven felt the subtle shift in her, the slight tension that spoke of her intrigue. He watched as her blue eyes, now darkened to stormy seas by dilated pupils, drank in the carnal displays with a curiosity that belied her former reticence. It was as if each scene whispered secrets only, they could understand, secrets of flesh and spirit mingling in a sacred dance.

Their shared journey through this night had peeled back layers of themselves they had never dared to shed in the light of day. The power dynamics they had toyed with, the relinquishing and seizing of control, had left indelible marks upon their souls. Here in this place, where desire reigned supreme, they had discovered hidden alcoves of their own hearts.

With a silent communion, their eyes met, conveying volumes in the briefest of glances. There was a reverence in Steven's gaze, a profound respect for the woman who walked beside him, transformed from the shy creature he knew into a siren of bold exploration. In return, Dana's eyes sparkled, reflecting not only the ambient light but also the fiery strength she had found within—a strength that had always been hers but had only now been set ablaze.

"Amazing," Steven murmured, the word barely more than a breath, yet it encapsulated the awe that swelled his chest. It was an homage to the beauty around them, yes, but more so to the beauty of what they had become together.

Dana's lips curved in a smile, soft and knowing. "Beyond," she replied, her voice a velvet caress against the din of unspoken yearnings. Her response was both an affirmation of the scenes that surrounded them and a declaration of the depths they had dived into, side by side.

Together, they continued their slow promenade towards the exit, the heaviness of the air imbued with the scent of musk and the warmth of skin—a symphony of senses that promised this chapter was merely the prelude to a richer story awaiting its telling.

iii

The night embraced Dana and Steven as they stepped through the threshold, trading the sultry haze of the club for the crisp clarity of the world outside. The cacophony of moans and sighs that had scored their journey within was now a whispering echo, dissipating into the cool air that caressed their flushed skin. The club's door swung shut with a muted thud, sealing away the fervor of intertwined bodies and unspoken promises, leaving them isolated under the vast canopy of the night.

Dana felt the change keenly, the brisk air drawing goosebumps across her flesh—a stark contrast to the heat that had coursed through her moments prior. She reveled in the sensation, a physical affirmation of the boundary they had crossed back into a realm where their shared secret thrummed between them with electric intimacy. Her hand, still entwined with Steven's, felt every tremble, every pulse that beat a rhythm of exhilarating satisfaction.

An impish breeze played with strands of her blonde hair, tossing them like golden threads catching the sparse light of the street lamps. In this newfound quietude, she found a voice that rang with authority over her own narrative of desire. Turning towards Steven, she allowed the confidence that swelled within her chest to crystallize into a gaze that held him captive. His dark eyes, still smoldering from the fires they had stoked together, met hers, and in that exchange, power dynamics shifted and danced like shadows upon their skin.

"Steven," she began, her voice a silken thread pulling at his attention. She leaned closer, her breath a warm whisper against the shell of his ear. "There is an ache," she confessed, the words charged with the weight of her anticipation, "a delicious ache that is now satisfied but begs to be stoked once more."

Her confession hung between them, a tantalizing promise that defied the night's chill. It was an invitation, one that beckoned him to reclaim and revel in the control he wielded, just as much as it was an assertion of her own power—the power to inspire such craving within him.

Dana's eyes never left Steven's, watching as her whispered intent unfurled within him. She saw the play of emotions—the flicker of surprise, the dawning of understanding, and the flare of renewed hunger—as clearly as if she'd traced them with her fingertip. In those eyes, she read volumes: the chapters of their exploration thus far, the pages yet to be turned, and the unwritten stories that awaited their inscription.

The silence around them was no longer empty but filled with the resonance of what lay ahead. Their connection, fortified by their escapades, stretched out before them, a path laden with the potential of pleasures yet to be seized. And in the quiet aftermath of revelation, Dana stood emboldened, a woman not just stepping out of the shadows but casting her own, her desires casting long lines into the future they would shape together.

Steven's pulse quickened, a symphony of blood and desire pounding in his ears as the implications of Dana's hushed words unfurled within him. A torrent of memories from their salacious escapades cascaded through his mind, reigniting an insatiable yearning that had merely simmered beneath the surface. Each recollection—a touch, a sigh, a forbidden pleasure—stoked the embers of his ardor into an inferno that demanded to be fed.

"What do you think we'll do next?" she breathed out, her voice a velvet caress against the shell of his ear. The weight of her anticipation settled upon him, heavy with promise.

In a seamless motion born of newfound urgency, Steven captured Dana's hand. His fingers interlaced with hers, an anchor in the whirlwind of sensation threatening to sweep them both away. He led her toward their car, each step a deliberate assertion of his eagerness to continue the dance of discovery they had begun. His grip was firm yet tender, a silent proclamation of his intent to guide them through the labyrinth of their desires.

A shiver danced down Dana's spine, a visceral response to the heat emanating from Steven's touch. It traced the curve of her back, igniting sparks along her skin as if his very fingertips were etching paths of fire.

She moved with him, her body an echo of his own hunger, a mirror reflecting the depth of their shared longing.

The night air wrapped around them, cool against their fevered skin, but it could not quell the warmth that radiated between them. They moved as one entity, drawn by an invisible thread spun from the fabric of their passion. As they neared the car, the world beyond their cocoon of desire fell away, leaving only the anticipation of what awaited them: a canvas blank and eager for the strokes of color they would paint upon it with the brush of their unbridled lust.

iv

The engine hummed a low, steady purr as Steven navigated the sleek car through the winding streets, away from the pulsating heart of the club. Inside the cocoon of the vehicle, the silence was a living thing—an electric current that thrummed between Dana and her husband, charged with the residue of their shared escapade.

Dana sat, her body pressed into the soft leather seat, feeling each turn in the road as a gentle reminder of the physical reality they'd left behind. The stillness was not empty but full, heavy with words unspoken yet understood, thick with the weight of a night that had forever altered the fabric of their intimacy.

The city lights blurred past, streaks of color that painted the darkness with fleeting impressions. Dana's gaze, however, remained inward, her thoughts cascading like a waterfall unfettered by hesitation or fear. They danced around the tantalizing possibilities that now lay before them, each one a promise of exploration, a testament to the depths they could reach within one another.

"Are you thinking what I'm thinking?" Steven broke the silence, his voice a velvet caress that seemed to stroke the air.

Dana turned toward him, her eyes glimmering pools of liquid desire. "I'm thinking of all the doors we've just opened," she whispered, her words a fragile thread weaving through the charged atmosphere. "And how eager I am to discover what lies beyond each threshold."

Steven reached over, his hand finding hers, fingers entwining with a familiarity that belied the newfound thrill pulsing through her veins. "Together," he affirmed, and the single word was imbued with so much more than agreement—it was a vow, an oath of companionship on the odyssey of desire they had embarked upon.

She squeezed his hand, reassured by its strength and the unspoken promise it held. Her mind continued to race, painting images of future rendezvous, each scenario more vivid and daring than the last. With every imagined whisper of touch, every shadow of pleasure that played across her thoughts, Dana felt herself drawn deeper into the intoxicating potential of their shared journey.

As the car slid into the silent embrace of their garage, the anticipation built within her was a tangible force, pulsing in time with her heartbeat. Tonight, they had tasted liberation; tomorrow, they would feast on the infinite flavors of their passion.

v

The car engine fell into silence as Steven pulled the key out of the ignition, the quiet hum of the night settling around them like a shroud. He turned to Dana, his eyes tracing the contours of her face, now soft in the moon's gentle caress. Each glance was an act of reverence, discovering anew the woman who had grown bolder before his very eyes.

"Home," he murmured, his voice low and husky with the remnants of desire that had yet to ebb away.

Dana nodded, her lips quirked in a secretive smile, one that held the echoes of their shared escapade. They stepped out of the car, their movements synchronized in the dance of familiarity, yet laced with the thrill of the unknown they'd just embraced. The tension between them crackled, an invisible thread binding them together even as they walked side by side.

Steven's gaze lingered on Dana as she locked the car, her fingers deftly pressing the button until the vehicle responded with a reassuring blink. In the simple gesture, there was a boldness that belied her usual reticence—a transformation wrought not just by the night's events but by the liberating journey upon which they had embarked.

Their footsteps tapped a slow rhythm against the pavement, the sound bouncing off the walls of the empty hallway that led to the sanctity of their bedroom. It was a hallowed path tonight, every echo a testament to the distance they had traveled—not just in miles, but in the spaces between their hearts.

"Tonight was..." Steven began, his voice trailing off as if words were too crude to encapsulate the profundity of their experience.

"An awakening," Dana finished for him, her voice steady despite the tremor he saw in her hands—nerves or excitement, it no longer mattered.

He reached for her hand, his fingers slipping between hers, locking them in a grip that spoke of possession and surrender all at once. Their eyes met, and something unspoken passed between them, a silent acknowledgment of the power they each yielded and submitted to in turn.

"We need to talk about it," Dana said as they paused before the door to their intimate sanctuary, her eyes alight with a fierce determination that set Steven's pulse racing anew. "Everything that happened, and what it means now."

"Agreed," he responded, pushing open the door and ushering her into the darkness of their bedroom, where the night's earlier fervor awaited, ready to be rekindled under the watchful eye of the moon that now peeked through their window, casting long, sensuous shadows across the room that promised to hold their whispered secrets until dawn.

ii

"Remember the way you looked at me?" Dana's voice was thick with yearning, her breath hitching as Steven's hand ventured lower, exploring the territory they had claimed together. "When I was with Marcus?"

"Every moment is etched here." Steven pressed a kiss just above her heart. "How could I forget?"

In that space of warmth and whispers, their encounter at the club lingered like a perfume, imbuing their senses with a potency that urged them to rediscover one another. The dim light threw shadows across their bodies, tantalizing hints of the shapes they formed together—shapes that spoke of an intimacy that had deepened in unexpected ways.

Dana's fingers wove through Steven's hair, tugging him closer until their lips met in a kiss that was both a question and an answer. It held the taste of their shared adventures, the tang of new territories on their tongues.

"Wherever this takes us," Dana said, her gaze locked with Steven's, "we go together."

"Always," he promised, sealing their pact with a kiss that spoke of endless horizons yet to be explored.

iii

Dana and Steven reclined on the king bed, enveloped in the warm ambiance created by the flickering daylight through the shades. Shadows danced across their features, enhancing the soft lines of contentment etched into their faces. The sensations from their night—skin against skin, whispers mingling with moans—still lingered, an electric hum beneath their settled calm.

In the quiet of the room, Dana turned to Steven, her gaze drinking in the man she had ventured through uncharted desires with. Her hand reached out, finding his in the dim light—a connection that felt as natural as breathing. Her fingers curled around his, a tender clasp that spoke volumes more than words ever could. She felt the familiar roughness of his skin, a contrast to her own, yet it was in these differences that their bond flourished.

"Steven," she began, her voice a velvet whisper that seemed almost sacred in the hush that surrounded them. "I can't begin to express... this journey, it's been more than I ever imagined." Her eyes, pools of sincerity and burgeoning confidence, held his steady gaze. "It has stretched me, pushed me to discover depths I didn't know I had. And in every step, I've felt us grow closer, our connection deepening in ways I never thought possible."

Dana's heart swelled with a gratitude that shimmered through her, a radiant energy that filled the space between them. There was awe in her tone as she continued, each word wrapped in the warmth of her affection for him. "Thank you for walking with me, side by side, through every fear, every thrill. It means the world to me."

Steven's response was silent, but his eyes, dark and full of his own reflections, echoed back to her an understanding that transcended language. In this shared silence, filled with the echoes of their adventure, they found a new layer of intimacy—the kind fashioned by souls laid bare and hearts entwined.

Steven's fingertips danced across Dana's forearm, sketching invisible symphonies on her flesh. The touch was light, reverent, as if he were both cherishing her skin and reading their story in its texture. He drew breath deeply, the air shared between them thick with the scent of vanilla candles and the lingering electricity of their recent escapades.

"Every moment with you there," he murmured, "was like stepping into a dream I never knew I wanted to live." His voice carried the weight of truths found in the dark, intimate corners of their explorations. "We've navigated through some stormy waters, haven't we? But look at us now—stronger, bolder... more ourselves than ever before."

Dana felt the resonance of his words thrumming in her veins, an affirmation of the growth that had branched out from the fertile ground of their mutual daring. She nuzzled into the crook of his neck, inhaling the familiar scent of him, now interwoven with memories of their sensory odyssey.

"Remember the first time?" she asked, a playful lilt in her tone that belied the enormity of the experience. "Watching you, watching me... There was this incredible charge in the air, potent enough to set our nerves alight."

Steven chuckled softly, the sound vibrating against her cheek. "How could I forget? It was exhilaration incarnate. To see you surrender to your desires, to witness your abandon—it was enthralling." His hand moved from her arm to cup her cheek, thumb caressing her jawline. "And yet, amid the fervor, it was the trust that floored me the most. The way we just... gave ourselves over to it, to each other."

Their gazes locked, twin flames flickering with the recognition of the profound trust that had taken root between them. In the reflection of each other's eyes, they saw the echoes of passion, of vulnerability, of the unspoken pacts they'd made beneath the gaze of strangers now turned confidants in the clandestine dance of desire.

"Trust," Dana echoed, her voice barely above a whisper. "It's the foundation, isn't it? Without it, none of this would have been possible." Her hand slid to rest atop his, pressing it closer to her face, savoring the strength and tenderness that emanated from his touch.

"Indeed," Steven agreed, his thumb tracing the line of her lips with a gentleness that belied the fervor of their previous encounters. "It's what makes us soar, even when we're standing still."

In the dim daylight, the lovers sat, wrapped not only in each other's arms but also in the profound realization of how far they'd journeyed and the infinite paths that lay ahead. The room around them held their whispers like precious secrets, the night outside extending an invitation to continue their dance of discovery.

iv

A shiver cascaded down Dana's spine as the memories unfurled like silk ribbons in her mind, each one a vibrant thread weaving through the tapestry of their shared escapades. Steven watched her face, illuminated by the soft glow of the morning sun, as it danced with shadows and light, reflecting a carousel of emotions.

"Remember the way your eyes locked with mine?" she said, her voice quivering with excitement. "In that instant, I felt like we were the only two people in the world, despite the sea of bodies around us."

Steven nodded, his chest swelling with a mix of vulnerability and awe. "It was electric," he murmured, recalling the pulsating energy that had surrounded them, the air thick with the scent of want and the sound of whispered promises. "Feeling you there with me, even as we ventured apart... it somehow brought us closer."

"New desires came alive within me," Dana confessed, her heart racing at the recollection. The soft light painted her curvy form with an ethereal touch, accentuating the flush that crept upon her cheeks. She marveled at how their boundaries had expanded, like the horizon at dawn, endless and full of color. "I never knew such depths within myself, such yearning for the unknown."

"Nor I," Steven admitted, his dark eyes reflecting a soul laid bare, a man who found strength in the unveiling of his own hidden cravings. Their love had deepened, not in spite of their exploration, but because of it – a tree rooting deeper into the earth even as it reached for the sky.

Then, Dana's gaze fell, and her voice grew soft as a secret shared between midnight and the coming light. "I was so afraid at first," she whispered, vulnerability seeping into her words. "Afraid of what it meant for us, for our future." Her hand trembled slightly in his, a delicate bird uncertain of its perch.

"Of losing me?" Steven asked gently, understanding the weight of her confession.

"Of losing us," she corrected, lifting her eyes to meet his once more. "But you... you were my rock, my anchor in a tempest of sensation and emotion." Gratitude resonated through her tone, a melody that sang of the support and understanding Steven had provided, unwavering as the Northern Star.

"Whatever fears you had, Dana, we faced them together," Steven said, his fingertips grazing her forearm in a silent vow of solidarity. "And look at us now, on the other side of those doubts, stronger and more connected than ever."

Their bodies leaned into each other naturally, like complementary notes in a symphony, as they found solace in their shared vulnerabilities and the strength they'd forged from them. In this quiet space between heartbeats, they were not just husband and wife but explorers returning home, their bond the precious treasure they'd unearthed along their journey.

Steven's voice, a soothing balm, broke the stillness of the room. "I won't pretend I didn't grapple with jealousy," he confessed, his thumb tracing the faint outline of a vein on Dana's wrist. "Watching you, wanting you, yet seeing you in another's embrace—it stirred a storm within me."

Dana's pulse fluttered beneath his touch, a silent echo of the chaos he described. "But through that tempest," Steven continued, "I found clarity. It forced us to navigate uncharted waters, communicating our fears and desires more openly than we ever had before."

"Openness," Dana echoed softly, her gaze locked with his. "It became our compass." She remembered the raw conversations, the nights spent dissecting the intricacies of their hearts—each word a step towards mutual understanding.

"Exactly," Steven affirmed, the corners of his eyes crinkling in shared remembrance. "It was trust that tethered us, even as we delved into the unknown. It gave us the courage to voice what we needed, to ask for consent, to respect one another's boundaries."

"Without judgment," she added, the weight of their past inhibitions lifting with each syllable. The lessons learned felt like revelations, carving out a sacred space where shame once resided. "We've embraced our desires, our true selves, without fear of reproach."

"Indeed," he said, a proud softness in his tone. "We've discovered power not in control, but in surrender, in giving ourselves permission to explore the depths of our passion."

Their journey, once fraught with trepidation, now stood as a testament to their metamorphosis—a transformation born of whispered fantasies and the bold pursuit of pleasure. Together, they had charted a course to a place where love and lust intertwined, forging an unbreakable chain of intimacy that bound them ever closer.

v

Dana leaned into Steven, her curves yielding to the contours of his body as they nestled together on the couch. The room's soft light danced across their skin, casting a warm glow that mirrored the heat emanating from their intertwined figures. With each breath, she inhaled the musky scent of him, a mixture of cologne and the residual excitement from their night at the club.

"Thank you," she whispered, her voice a soft caress against the shell of his ear. "For every moment of vulnerability, for every leap into the unknown. For us."

Steven's hand traced the arc of her spine, fingertips meandering with purposeful languor. "It's us who have made this journey so profound," he replied, his tone imbued with reverence. His touch was both an exploration and a promise, a silent vow that mapped out the uncharted territories of their shared desire.

Their gazes locked, a silent exchange that spoke volumes of the gratitude swelling in their chests. Each memory, a brushstroke on the canvas of their relationship, painted images of growth and boundless affection. They had been sculpted by shared experiences, molded by pleasures once shrouded in trepidation but now celebrated in the light of their love.

"Let's keep pushing the edges of our world," Dana said, her voice brimming with the thrill of anticipation. Her fingers laced through his, a tangible sign of their unity. "I want to explore every desire with you, Steven. To discover places within ourselves we never knew existed."

"Every boundary we cross, we'll cross together," he affirmed, his words a steady anchor in the vast sea of their passions. "Our connection—this bond—is what I cherish most." In the silence that followed, his pledge resonated between them, a declaration that spanned beyond the physical realm into the very essence of their beings.

"Always," she breathed, sealing their commitment with a kiss that smoldered with the intensity of their past explorations and the fervency for those yet to come. Their lips met with the confidence of two souls intertwined, emboldened by the challenges they had surmounted and the intimacy they had wrought from courage and candor.

In the sanctuary of their embrace, Dana and Steven found not just solace, but an exhilarating freedom—the kind only true lovers can forge in the crucible of their mutual desires.

vi

Steven drew Dana closer, their bodies folding together like the pages of a well-thumbed novel. In the aftermath of their passionate declarations, they settled into a comfortable silence, each heartbeat a soft murmur in the quiet room. The light cast a warm, amber hue over their entwined figures, painting them in an intimate portrait that spoke more eloquently than words ever could.

Dana's head rested against Steven's chest; her ear tuned to the steady rhythm of his heart—a reassuring drumbeat that underscored the gravity of their shared future. His arms enveloped her, the strength in his embrace a testament to the fortress of trust they had built brick by brick. There was a sense that for Dana and Steven, the present moment stretched out infinitely.

"Can you feel it?" Dana's whisper was barely audible, a feather's touch against the fabric of the evening. "That tingling sense of adventure just on the horizon?"

"Like electricity in the air before a storm," Steven replied, his voice a low thrum that vibrated through her. "It's invigorating."

Their journey thus far had been a tapestry woven with threads of exploration, each color a different shade of their love and longing. The experiences at the swinger club had opened doors they'd only dared to peek through before. Now, emboldened, they stood ready to step across those thresholds hand in hand.

"Remember the rules we set for ourselves?" he asked, his breath stirring the blonde tendrils of her hair. "We'll keep them as our anchor, no matter where the tides take us."

"Always," she responded, her fingers tracing the contours of his forearm, feeling the play of muscle beneath skin. "Our compass."

"Tomorrow," Steven murmured as if reading her thoughts, "we'll chart a course to unexplored waters. Maybe back to the club, or perhaps a new challenge altogether."

"Either way," Dana breathed out, her anticipation a tangible thing between them, "it's another chapter in our story."

Indeed, as they lingered in the cocoon of their embrace, the world outside faded away, leaving only the promise of what was to come. The scent of melted wax and the vestiges of their earlier fervor lingered in the air, mingling to forge a signature fragrance of their union.

"Whatever it is," she said, her tone laced with conviction, "we'll face it together."

"Always," he echoed once more, sealing the vow with a kiss pressed to her forehead. It was a kiss of partnership, of power shared and wielded with mutual respect—a declaration that no matter the trials they would encounter, their bond would remain unbroken.

EPILOGUE

I t had been a few weeks since their thrilling adventures at the club. The rush of arousal, the thrill of breaking societal barriers, and the sense of adventure slowly faded into the mundane routine of everyday life. Simple tasks like wiping the kitchen counter or changing over the laundry became more commonplace than the sensual and erotic dance performed at the club.

But as Dana was lost in her thoughts while doing one of these mundane tasks, she was suddenly jolted back to reality by a notification on her phone. She glanced down to see a simple message from Richard:

"Dana, it's Richard. I would like to see you and continue our exploration."

The memories of their time together flooded back like a raging river, overwhelming her with desire and longing for more.

In a burst of hope and excitement, she called out, "Steven, I need you to take a look at this!"